Also available from General Paperbacks

Dick North

General
— PAPERBACKS —
Toronto, Canada

The
Mad Trapper
of
Rat River

Published in 1991 by
General Paperbacks
30 Lesmill Road
Toronto, Canada
M3B 2T6
Published in hardcover in 1972 by Macmillan of Canada
First Laurentian Library edition, 1976
Reprinted in 1979, 1980, 1982, 1984

First Macmillan Paperbacks edition 1987
Reprinted 1988
Published by arrangement with
Macmillan of Canada
A Division of Canada Publishing Corporation

Canadian Cataloguing in Publication Data

North, Dick
The mad trapper of Rat River
First published (1969) under title : The saga of the mad trapper of
Rat River.
ISBN 0-7736-7307-5
1. Johnson, Albert, d. 1932.   2. Royal Canadian Mounted
Police.
3. Criminals — Northwest Territories — Biography.   I. Title.
FC4172.1.J6N67 1991   364.1'523'092   C90-095816-2
    F1060.9.J6N67 1991

Cover Design: Craig Allen
Cover Illustration: Joe Morse

Printed and bound in the United States of America

Dedicated to
Jean, Ed, and Lee

Contents

Illustrations

Acknowledgments

This book would not have been possible without the aid and support of Bert Giesbrect, Toronto-Dominion Bank; Cal Miller, Capital Hotel; Dave Robertson; Ken Shortt, *Yukon News;* the Royal Canadian Mounted Police; the staff of the Yukon Territorial Library; Perry Creighton, Bank of Commerce; Bob Yaskell; Fred Francais; Jane Smith; and Barbara Tennison.

Cpl. Al Pitt of the Identification Section of the Royal Canadian Mounted Police was invaluable for his work on the various blow-ups of Nelson's photo at Ross River.

S. W. Horrall, historian for the R.C.M.P. in Ottawa, was a consistent and patient source of information, as was Staff Sgt. Terry Shaw, editor of the *R.C.M.P. Quarterly.*

I would like to thank Inspector Guy Marcoux for his assistance and interest, as well as the Edmonton and Ottawa laboratories of the R.C.M.P.

Irving Tyson, of Juneau, Alaska, was also of great help.

Additional Mounties who were of assistance are Cpl. Dan Wheeler, with information and photos covering the Old Crow area, and Sgt. Paul Robin, who contributed much in the way of description of Mountie patrols in northern Yukon.

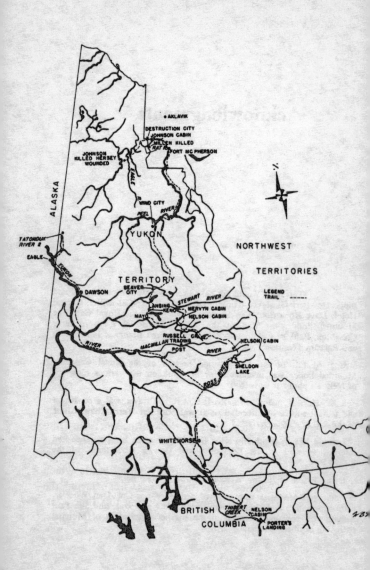

Introduction

        This is the true story of one of the most fantastic confrontations in the history of the North American frontier. One man, Albert Johnson, defied a combined force of white trappers, Indians, and men of the Royal Canadian Mounted Police in a forty-eight-day running battle which ranged for 150 miles along the Arctic Circle during the winter of 1931-2. The temperature during this time averaged forty below zero. Exhibiting incredible fortitude, courage, woodsmanship, and fighting ability, Johnson was to engage in four shoot-outs with his pursuers, seriously wounding two men and killing a third before he was finally killed on the Eagle River, Yukon Territory, February 17, 1932.

Courage and stamina were not traits which were limited to the fugitive. Incredible feats of perseverance and bravery were everyday occurrences with the pursuers as well as the pursued. The flying of Wop May; the dog mushing of Constables R. G. McDowell, Lazarus Sittichinli, and Joe Bernard; the persistence of trackers Karl Gardlund, Noel Verville, Const. Edgar Millen, and Sgt. R. F. Riddell; the boldness of Knut Lang; and the courage of the wounded men, Sgt. Earl Hersey and Const. Alfred King, were to justify the nickname given the fifty-four-day conflict—"The Arctic Circle War". For these reasons the incident has earned a permanent niche in the history of the Royal Canadian Mounted Police.

If any single episode of the North American frontier represented the end of one era and the beginning of another, it was this. For the first time a plane was used by the Royal Canadian Mounted Police in tracking a man down. Also for the first time, a two-way radio was utilized in a tactical manner in bringing a man to justice in the Arctic. As a direct consequence of the battle, the medium of radio took on a degree of importance in news broadcasting that it had never possessed before. People purchased radios for no other reason than to keep up with the news of the pursuit of the trapper. Still other consequences of the Johnson event were the establishment of registered trap lines in the Yukon and Northwest Territories, as well as the inception of the Air Wing of the R.C.M.P.

There is more to the story than the "war" in the Arctic. A photo, uncovered after forty years, has been tentatively identified by some as including Albert Johnson when he was alive and going under the name Arthur Nelson in the Yukon Territory and northern British Columbia. During his five-year sojourn in these areas Nelson was to remain aloof, though indications are that he was on the trail of the "Lost McHenry Gold Mine" of the Mackenzie Mountains, the "Lost McLeod Mine" of the infamous land of death known as Headless Valley in the region of the South Nahanni River, and possibly the "Lost Porcupine Mine" of the Porcupine River in the northern Yukon.

Albert Johnson was an irrepressible traveller who walked from British Columbia to the Arctic Ocean. Along his itinerary men were to vanish mysteriously, though to this day no irrefutable proof has been presented establishing a connection between Johnson and the vanishing men.

Johnson's travels were marked by settlements which have long since become ghost towns. Porter's Landing, Laketon, Husky Dog Town, Lansing, Russell Creek, Fraser Falls, Beaver City, Wind City, La Pierre House, and Destruction City were settlements which though obscure have an important place in the history of the north country.

The story of Albert Johnson is one of a man of mystery. Though the author has tentatively established the fact that he lived in the Yukon as Arthur Nelson and has traced him back to Dease Lake in northern British Columbia, there the trail ends. Johnson's point of origin has never been established. In a sense this is the story of two men, Albert Johnson and Arthur Nelson, and in order to avoid confusion the author has divided the book accordingly.

Now, almost forty years after the occurrence of the incident, Albert Johnson has taken his part in the folklore of the north country. A song has been written about him, and also a poem. Seldom can his name be mentioned without causing an argument. Was he to be pitied or damned? As the years go by, the legend grows, and it becomes difficult to separate fact from fiction. This story is an attempt to gather the facts before they become lost in the annals of time. It is one of the most interesting sagas in the history of the Arctic and the vast, forested region called the Sub-Arctic—a tough and unforgiving country.

Prologue

THE MAN WAS five feet nine inches tall. He had blond hair and pale blue eyes. He weighed 175 pounds, with legs like tree stumps; his neck and shoulders were as powerful as a caribou bull's. His name was Arthur Nelson. He unslung the two rifles he carried over his two-hundred-pound pack. He put one rifle into the snow. It was a Winchester .22. He hefted the other rifle in his hands and quietly racked a shell into the breech. It was a 30-30 Model 99 Featherweight "take-down" Savage, and made up in muzzle velocity what it lacked in size. Slowly, the rugged, clear-eyed man knelt down into the snow. Unseen, he eyed the figure of a man following his trail. He wondered who would be following him here, above McQuesten Flats fifteen miles north of Keno, Yukon Territory. It was May 7, 1931, and he was heading to the Beaver River, and then across the Wernecke Mountains to the Arctic slope, and from there down north to the Porcupine country. He wanted to be alone and was ready to ensure that he would be. Slowly, he raised the rifle to his shoulder. Ten more steps and the man would be close enough. Nelson put his index finger through the trigger-guard of the rifle. He counted nine, eight, seven, six, five—suddenly the stranger stopped, looked around briefly, and then turned and started back the way he had come. Nelson brought the Savage down from his shoulder. He had seen that the man wore the chocolate-brown drill parka of the Royal Canadian Mounted Police. Nelson shrugged his shoulders and slung the two rifles over his pack and continued north. He was never seen again.

Former Royal Canadian Mounted Police Corporal Thomas Coleman, now retired from the British Columbia Department of Highways in Atlin, B.C., still wonders what might have happened if he had kept following Nelson's trail through the snow on May 7, 1931. He never forgot the date because it was his twenty-seventh birthday. He had been north to the Silver Hill area and had counted William Langham, Christopher Williams, and Thomas Morwick while taking the census. He was mushing back to Keno when he came across tracks which abruptly led off the trail. Coleman tied his dog team to a tree and stepped off into the deep snow to follow the trail made by the other man. Since the other man was not wearing snow-shoes, the Mountie did not think that the man would go very far. "Probably hunting," Coleman thought as he struggled through snow made sloppy by the warm winds of spring. He followed the fresh trail for four hundred yards, and then decided to turn around and go back. More than likely he had already included the individual in the census, or if not, he would count him when he returned down the trail later. Yet, there were two aspects of the situation which puzzled him. One was the possibility that the man might have run off the trail to avoid him, and the other was his speed in getting out of sight. Coleman doubted if the man could have heard his dog team coming from more than a quarter of a mile away, yet he had managed to jump off the trail and disappear in the space of time it took Coleman to go four hundred yards downhill by dog team over a beaten trail. The Mountie speculated that whoever the man was, he was in tremendous physical condition.

Coleman made his way back to his team and then mushed eight miles to where John Kinman and Leon "Snoose" Erickson were camped on a small stream which drains out of Hanson Lakes. Here, he met Kinman fishing by the bridge which crosses the stream.

"You see anyone go by here recently, John?" Coleman asked.

Kinman nodded. "Yes, some guy was carrying a pack that would break the back of a mule. He was carrying two rifles, a 250-3000 Savage and a .22. He wasn't very friendly though. I said hello, and he just mumbled something I couldn't hear and walked on by."*

Coleman thanked Kinman for his information and went on to Keno. He kept thinking about the tracks he had followed. Something was not right. Two weeks earlier he had walked into the Northern Commercial Company store in Keno and met a stranger face to face. The man had such a hard look about him that Coleman asked the storekeeper, Dick O'Loane, who he was.

*Model 99 30-30 Featherweight Savage and 250-3000 look the same.

"I don't know," O'Loane said, "though I told him that you were taking the census and would need to get his name. He told me that he had already been counted down in Mayo."

Coleman thought about this when he returned to Keno. He picked up the telephone and called Constable Don Perks in Mayo, and asked whether Perks had included the stranger in his census report.

"No," Perks told him, "I haven't counted one person that I didn't already know."

The stranger and the man who had passed John Kinman had certainly been the same man. He had eluded census takers, but why? Coleman had other duties to perform, and he shrugged off the incident, but in his mind a nagging question persisted about the man's identity.

Big John MacDonald was another who wondered who the stranger was. MacDonald was a friendly giant of a man who was generally conceded to be the toughest individual in a region of tough men—the Yukon Territory. MacDonald, who was popularly known as "Hard Rock", was offered five dollars by the stranger if he would show him the route north. "Hard Rock" was somewhat surprised by the offer for directions which he gladly gave for nothing. This, and the strange attitude of the transient, perplexed him. Why would anyone offer to pay for information in a region where the hospitality of the people was taken for granted?

Still another person who was to wonder about the stranger was Bud Fisher, who at that time operated a transportation business in Mayo. Several weeks before Coleman met Nelson, Fisher had given the man a ride from Keno to Mayo. "I would say that he either came in from Lansing by way of Mayo Lake, or he had been in the direction of Great Bear Lake and come from there." Fisher said the man purchased supplies in Mayo and then walked back toward Keno. Fisher never saw the man again either.

*The
Mad Trapper
of
Rat River*

Part One

Albert Johnson

One

The Stranger

On July 7, 1931, Indian brothers William and Edward Snowshoes of Fort McPherson, Northwest Territories, were paddling up the Peel River in their canoe when they came across the camp of a white man. He was sitting under a mosquito-bar. One of the Indians nudged the other and said, "He must be Paul Nieman's brother. Paul said he come here soon. His name is Albert Johnson."

One of the Snowshoes brothers then hailed the camp,

calling out the name "Albert Johnson". The shadowy figure stirred under the mosquito net before answering. "What do you want?" he asked.

"Are you Albert Johnson?" Edward asked matter-of-factly.

The stranger said he was, and then asked the brothers if he was on the Porcupine River. They said no, that he was on the Peel River, adding that the Porcupine River was a hundred miles to the west. The newcomer shook his head in disgust and sat back under his shelter. William and Edward realized that the man was finished talking. They shrugged their shoulders and shoved their boat out into the current. The two men continued up river to where they tended their gill nets, and later returned to Fort McPherson. They reported the stranger's presence and in so doing apparently used the name Albert Johnson. However, this man was not Paul Nieman's brother-in-law.

Paul Nieman was not at McPherson at the time, though he had been in and out of the northern trading post for four years. He is still remembered for his great help in nursing the Loucheux Indians through the disastrous flu epidemic of 1928. An Albert Johnson had married Nieman's sister, Frieda. The Indians were particularly cognizant of the name Albert Johnson because Nieman had regaled them with stories of the "great fire-eating monster" which his brother-in-law, a fireman with the Canadian National Railways, drove across the prairies. Few, if any, had ever seen a locomotive. Nieman's brother-in-law had occasionally mentioned that he would like to visit the lower Mackenzie area to take a trip over his trap line; thus the reason for Nieman's telling the local residents of the possibility of Albert Johnson's visit.

Fort McPherson, N.W.T., was originally called Peel's River House. It was founded in 1840, fourteen years after Sir John Franklin discovered the Peel River. In 1848 the Hudson's Bay Company established a trading post there and the settlement received its current name. Four years later Loucheux Indians moved to Fort McPherson from their camp on the Peel River opposite Stony Creek. The name *Loucheux* was a slang term used to describe the local Indians by the early voyageurs, the name meaning "slant eyes" or "slant-eyed people". The Indians are Athabaskan and are directly related to the Apache and Navajo of the American southwest. They also have a striking resemblance to Japanese.

Two decades after the building of the Hudson's Bay trading post, Robert Macdonald became the first Anglican missionary among the Indians at Fort McPherson. He married a Loucheux woman, and shortly thereafter put himself to the task of translating the Bible into the Loucheux (Athabaskan) language. His son, Neil Macdonald, now (1972) in his eighties and resident postmaster of Old Crow, Y.T., remembers his father asking his mother to repeat Loucheux words over and over again as he sought to spell them phonetically. When Macdonald had mastered the language sufficiently, he concentrated on teaching the natives English. Thus, by the early 1900s a fair number of Indians could speak and write English.

On July 9, 1931, Albert Johnson walked in to purchase supplies from Northern Traders Ltd. in Fort McPherson. W. W. Douglas sold the visitor a 16-gauge Iver Johnson single-barrel shotgun and twenty-five shells. Douglas noted that the new man was an ideal customer. Said Douglas, "He knew what he wanted, bought it with no hesitation, and appeared to have plenty of cash." Douglas described the stranger as being about five feet nine inches tall, with light brown hair and "cold blue eyes". He also noted that the man was a very taciturn individual.

The quiet man returned upstream and set up his tent across the river from Abe Francis's fishing camp. He remained there almost three weeks. During this time Francis talked with him on several occasions and recalled that

Johnson each time seemed to try to hide his face and appeared to be a very nervous person. One day a storm hit McPherson. Andrew Kunnezi, who in 1914 had guided a Royal North West Mounted Police patrol from Dawson City to Fort McPherson and fifty-five years later led a Northwest Territories centennial dog-sled trip from Fort McPherson to Dawson City, recalled walking to Johnson's tent with some others. He asked Johnson if he would like to come in out of the storm and stay with them at the post. Johnson said no and flipped down the tent flap.

On another occasion, William Firth opened the door to the Hudson's Bay post one morning and found Johnson sitting in front of the store with a tobacco can in his hands. He purchased over seven hundred dollars' worth of supplies which he paid for from cash that was carried in the can. Firth, too, said that Johnson was a good customer. He learned that the stranger's name was Albert Johnson, and that he was planning either to establish a trap line along Rat River or to follow its portage route over the Richardson Mountains west to the Yukon Territory.

In a settlement as small as Fort McPherson, Johnson was not to go unnoticed. Bishop W. A. Geddes of the Anglican Church reported his presence to Inspector Alexander Eames, commander of the Western Arctic Sub-District of the Royal Canadian Mounted Police. Geddes's trip to Aklavik was routine, as was Eames's resultant request to Constable Edgar "Spike" Millen of the Arctic Red River detachment to interview Johnson on his next trip to McPherson.

One day when John Robert was alone and tending the counter in the Northern Traders store, Johnson purchased a few items and queried, "Are there any white men trapping between Arctic Red River and the Peel River?" Robert shook his head and said, no, there were not.

On July 21, Const. Millen met Johnson at Fort McPherson when the trapper was purchasing more supplies. Millen as a matter of course asked Johnson where he had come from. This was not done out of idle curiosity. The depression was in full swing. Many men were heading north into the bush to trap and hunt who were obviously unqualified for such a strenuous occupation. When they got into trouble it caused considerable difficulty for the R.C.M.P. and others to get them out of it. Thus, the Mounties strove to make sure newcomers were properly equipped and knew what they were doing before they went into an area. Casual surveillance and questioning were usually all that were needed to satisfy the Mountie as to an individual's capabilities.

Johnson told Millen that he had spent the previous year on the prairies and had come into the Arctic by the Mackenzie River system. Millen was aware that the trapper had come down the Peel River, and doubted Johnson's story. However, he did not press the matter. There were many men in the back country who were reticent about elaborating on their itinerary. This particularly applied to prospectors and trappers because it was to their own self-interest not to tell others where they had been. They were also quite aware in those days that Mounties often prospected and ran trap lines in their spare time.

Const. Millen advised Johnson that if he did elect to remain and trap in the area, he would have to purchase a trapper's licence from the police, and that he might save himself a trip to the nearest police post at Arctic Red River if he purchased one now.

A week later Johnson bought a small twelve-foot canoe from Abe Francis. That same day he walked into W. W. Douglas's trading post and purchased some more supplies. John Robert was again clerking and asked Johnson if he would like to purchase a small outboard motor for his boat. "No," Johnson said and flexed his arms, "these are good enough for me. I'm not crazy yet." He then walked down to the river and launched his canoe, which he paddled downstream.

He missed the Rat River and a short time later floated

7

by Arthur Blake's post at the confluence of the Husky and Peel rivers, only to return four days later to ask Blake the way to the Rat. Blake told him that one way was to go back up the Peel a few miles and then up the south branch of the Rat from that point. Johnson did not take that route, showing that he knew there were two other branches of the river which were navigable. The middle Rat, quite commonly used, flowed into the Husky River several miles north of Blake's post, and about seventy-two miles south of Aklavik. The third branch was called the north Rat.

The three branches of the Rat River drift away from the main stream after it flows out of the Richardson Mountains. As a consequence, no matter which branch a man took he still had to face the toughest part of the stream. It was a hand-lining proposition under extremely difficult conditions.* Indians and, later, frontiersmen have used the Rat River portage for centuries in their journeys to the Porcupine River and westward to the Yukon River. Few were ever heard to say that the Rat River portage was an easy trip.

Three men who adequately attested to the difficulties of the portage were "Kansas" Gilbert, "Slim" Jackson, and John Campbell. These three men successfully negotiated the portage while on the way to the Klondike in 1898, but it took them twenty-two days to go forty-eight miles. During this struggle it once took them one entire day to go one mile, and the next day to go two more miles. Elizabeth Page told of the difficulties the men experienced in her book *Wild Horses and Gold*. For example, on July 21, 1898, the three stampeders spent the entire day on tracking lines hauling their boat up the Rat.† Most of the second day, the men hauled their supply-laden craft up the crooked channels through a virtual jungle of willows crowding the

---

*Hand-lining means to pull a water craft upstream by using a rope.
†Tracking is a term used in describing the method of pulling a boat upstream by using hand-lines.

banks of the river. While this was going on they had to suffer attacks from "venomous" mosquitoes, and savage "bulldogs" (flies which were armed with a sting like a "red hot dagger").

Toward evening of the second day these men came to the beginning of fast water, at the confluence of the Rat and the Longstick rivers. A conglomeration of argonauts had gathered at this point to unload and rebuild their boats for the rugged portage, principally because the boats used for the Mackenzie trip were much too large for tracking up the Rat. As a result of this activity, a regular tent city was built along the banks of the river. Flotsam from boats already shortened, and from other craft which had been wrecked farther upstream in the rapids of the river, was discernible all over the place. The three men became aware of the failures of less experienced men, and they noted that someone had posted a sign at the camp naming it "Destruction City".

Gilbert, Jackson, and Campbell continued on over the pass to the Yukon, arriving that summer, but many others were not so fortunate. Forced by necessity to remain on the Rat River that winter, about forty people suffered through the cold months at Destruction City and Shack Town, another settlement located at the head of the pass.

Albert Johnson followed the same route and chose a point approximately eight miles upstream from the site of Destruction City to build his cabin. He placed the structure on a promontory which afforded him a good view on three sides. His cabin was located south of the winter trail which ran through a series of lakes cutting off a bend of the Rat River. This location also happened to be in the vicinity of the trap lines of three men—William Vittrekwa, Jacob Drymeat, and William Nerysoo.

The rest of the summer and the fall Johnson spent building and preparing his 8' x 10' cabin for the winter trapping season, and hunting meat for his food stock. On one trip to the headwaters of the Rat River at Loon Lake, he met James Hogg, who trapped the upper reaches of the Bell River, a tributary of the Porcupine which flows west to the Yukon River. He was civil to Hogg, but non-committal about his presence in the region.

Two

Rat River

CHRISTMAS WAS A colourful festival at Arctic Red River. The Loucheux people often joined the whites in parties and dances during the holiday season. The natives would dress accordingly, donning mukluks, and shirts and parkas which displayed some of the finest beadwork produced by any people in the world. Both races joined in the fun and sometimes the celebration would go on for days. However, a damper was to be cast on the 1931 Christmas.

Little was heard about Albert Johnson until December 25, when William Nerysoo walked into the Arctic Red River post for Christmas and complained to Const. Millen that Johnson had been springing his traps and hanging them on trees in the vicinity of Rat River.

The day after Christmas, Millen ordered Const. Alfred "Buns" King and Special Const. Joe Bernard to mush to Johnson's cabin and question the man about the traps being sprung.

It was bitterly cold when the two men set out with two dog teams. A raw wind nipped at the men as their teams raced thirty miles westward through forty-below-zero temperatures to reach Fort McPherson. That night they stayed with Hudson's Bay trader John Firth and his son, William. Firth invited them to come back for a New Year's Eve party, which was something not to be missed, as the old trader was known to throw the finest parties in the north country. The two men said they would try to make it.

The next morning King and Bernard turned their teams northward, going down the Peel River. The temperature was again under forty below zero with a prevailing wind from the north, a nagging reminder that they were travelling abroad in a land which can be the most inhospitable on earth. The Arctic is a region of violent extremes where seventy-five-below-zero temperatures are not uncommon. In the winter, watercourses freeze and become arteries of travel with all their inherent dangers. One error in judgment can send a man and his dog team through rotten ice to disappear forever in the frigid waters beneath him. A musher can suddenly find himself wading knee deep in slush ice, though even to an experienced eye the slush may have been unnoticeable. If he is not able to start a fire immediately to dry out his clothes, frostbite can result, which, if severe enough, can lead to permanent injury or even death. The spectre of death is man's constant companion on the trail in the Arctic. At sixty below zero a man can break or mistakenly burn the handle of an axe and freeze to death because he cannot build a fire. A broken snowshoe, a sprained ankle, or lost mittens can so incapacitate an arctic traveller that he must make camp or die on the trail.

In winter the darkness is a continuous thing which seems to accentuate the great silence which envelops the vast snow-covered land. In such a void, the raucous gurgle of a raven plays on one's ears like an enchanted melody and the forlorn cry of a timber wolf is a welcome interruption to an otherwise silent world.

King and Bernard journeyed twenty-five miles to the mouth of the Rat before making a brush camp. They cut spruce boughs for a ground cover and threw up a tarp for a windbreak. The two men chained their dogs to trees, fed them, and built a fire. They cooked their evening meal, and rolled up in their sleeping bags with the fire for companionship and the grandeur of the northern lights for a ceiling. Life, though dangerous, is not without its compensations in the Arctic.

The next morning King and Bernard started up the Rat River. Visiting trappers' cabins on routine patrols was nothing new to Const. King. He had joined the Force in 1926, and had volunteered for northern service. Previous postings had included the isolated post at Old Crow, Yukon Territory. This was located on the Porcupine River about 250 miles directly west and across the Richardson Mountains from where he now drove his sled. King had also served in Dawson City, the capital of the Yukon Territory, and had participated in dog and horse patrols through the famous Klondike region. He was known to be one of the ruggedest men at "G" Division Headquarters. He had a superb physique, and few, if any, of his fellow Mounties could defeat him in a wrestling match.

King and Bernard mushed to the junction of the Longstick and Rat rivers. Here they travelled south for eight miles following the course of the river where it tumbles down out of the Richardson Mountains. They arrived at Albert Johnson's cabin at noon, December 28. The shack was about eight by ten feet and made out of spruce logs. King's experienced eyes noticed snowshoes in front of the small dwelling, and smoke coming out of the stovepipe. In the time-accustomed manner of the North, he shouted a greeting. Receiving no acknowledgement, he snowshoed up to the four-foot-high door and knocked. "Mr. Johnson my name is Constable King," said the Mountie. "I have received a complaint about you interfering with a nearby trap line and would like to ask you a few questions." He received no answer. Puzzled, King looked toward the twelve-inch-square window which was immediately to the right of the door and observed Johnson staring at him from behind a burlap sack. As soon as Johnson saw that King was looking at him, he flipped the sack back over the window.

King, with his experience in dealing with men in the bush, sensed trouble. It was unnatural for an individual to ignore a knock on the door or a greeting when he lived in such a degree of isolation. Under normal circumstances the traveller on the trail could expect to be asked in to have tea and to spend the night if time allowed. The constable thought possibly the man might be wary of him because he represented the law, so he again patiently explained his mission and spent almost an hour waiting for the trapper to make an appearance. However, not only would the trapper not come out, he ventured not a word during the entire time King and Bernard were there.

King realized that he could do nothing more until he acquired a search warrant. He decided that the best thing he could do was to go eighty miles down the Husky River to Aklavik and report the incident to Inspector Eames, commander of the Mounties' Arctic sub-division. King figured he would need reinforcements, and there would be men available at Aklavik where none were to spare at Arctic Red River.

The two men went half the distance to Aklavik that day and then completed their trip on December 29. Eames agreed that it would be a good idea to reinforce King and Bernard. He issued a warrant and assigned Const. R. G. McDowell and Special Const. Lazarus Sittichinli to make the trip back to the cabin with King and Bernard. They left early on the morning of December 30 and travelled fast, one of the reasons being they hoped to take care of the Johnson call and then mush on to Fort McPherson in time to celebrate New Year's Eve at Firth's. When they broke camp on December 31, they did not bother to eat breakfast because they felt it would take too much time.

They reached Johnson's cabin at about noon. King left McDowell and the other two men by the river bank and walked to within hailing distance of the cabin. He shouted: "Are you there, Mr. Johnson?" There was no answer. King had noted smoke coming out of the cabin's stovepipe. He knew Johnson was at home. King shouted again and said he had a warrant and would have to force in the door if Johnson did not open it. Johnson remained silent.

Expecting trouble, King approached the door from the side away from the window. He turned partially sideways, extended his left arm, and knocked on the door with the back of his left hand. Immediately a shot rang out, which, in the frigid cold, sounded as if a bomb had exploded. A puff of wood and dust indicated that the shot had come through the door. It hit King and knocked him into the snow, but he managed to recover enough to crawl to the river bank. McDowell and the two special constables fired a series of shots into the cabin to keep Johnson down, and pulled the wounded man over the river bank. At the same time the trapper returned fire, the slugs narrowly missing McDowell. McDowell, Bernard, and Sittichinli lashed King to one of the sleds and started their historic dash to save

King's life. They had eighty miles to go. Their dogs were tired, having already run for half a day. The temperature was forty below zero, and twenty-knot winds had blown up. Wind is the bane of mushers because drifting snow fills up their back trail. This means they have to perform the excruciating task of breaking trail all over again. The musher curses the wind with the vehemence of a drill sergeant addressing a stumbling recruit.

Wind also creates another unpleasant situation for the musher, and especially for a passenger. This is the danger of frostbite. A twenty-knot wind at forty below zero will plunge the skin-freezing chill factor to ninety below. Such a gale will slash the face of a man, turning his features into a white mantle of frost with each laboured breath. Even with a parka, fluid from a running nose freezes in a man's nostrils, and an ice film will collect on his eyelids. His cheeks will freeze and eyes close if he does not constantly warm them with his hands. Consequently, King's comrades had to stop and rub his face to prevent frostbite, but at the same time could not spare precious minutes to rest. In only a few hours darkness had enveloped the trail as they plunged northwards toward Aklavik.

There was still another obstacle which Bernard, McDowell, and Sittichinli had to overcome. This was the winding trail which continuously rose and fell over steep banks as it crossed and recrossed portages of the Husky River. The three men and two teams went on mile after mile, hour after hour, patiently lowering and then hoisting King over precipitous inclines as they broke trail in their race against death. They could average no better than four miles an hour. This seems slow compared to the speed of a racing team which can do better than fifteen miles an hour, but then racing teams are not burdened with a load, and do not have to break trail, and have not travelled for one hundred miles before their race.

Mile after mile, men and dogs bent their heads into the biting wind while they pushed their way toward Aklavik.

It took them twenty hours to reach Aklavik, which was good time considering the difficulties they had had to overcome. Once there, King was rushed to the settlement's small hospital. Resident Doctor J. A. Urquhart found that the bullet had passed through the left side of King's chest and had come out the right side. The slug had missed any vital organs. King, who was in excellent physical condition, recovered quickly under the tender care of nurses McCabe and Brownlee, and was up and around in three weeks.

Inspector Eames had a total of eleven men under his command in the Aklavik sub-division. There were a corporal, six constables, and one special constable at Aklavik. The other police post, at Arctic Red River, was run by two constables and a special constable. There was no police post at Fort McPherson, though at one time there had been as many as nine policemen stationed there. Another federal detachment located at Aklavik was the Royal Canadian Corps of Signals established in 1925. The Signals men were to prove invaluable in their assistance in apprehending Johnson.

Eames chose a force of nine men and forty-two dogs to go after Johnson. The party that left Aklavik on January 4, 1932, consisted of Inspector Eames, Constable McDowell, Special Constables Bernard and Sittichinli, and Ernest Sutherland, Karl Gardlund, and Knut Lang. (Lang was later elected to the Territorial Council of the Northwest Territories.) Eames sent word by the Signals' radio station "UZK" for Millen to meet him at the mouth of the Rat River.

Two days later, the police posse stopped briefly at Blake's post and found Const. Edgar Millen and an Indian guide, Charley Rat, waiting for them. Millen was presumably the only member of the party who had ever seen Johnson face to face. Blake had seen him, but was not to join the search until later. At Blake's, Eames purchased twenty pounds of dynamite.

The next day, the police and deputies journeyed to the

17

junction of the Longstick and Rat rivers and made camp. At this point, Johnson's cabin was roughly eight miles away. That night they decided that the best course to take was to circle Johnson's cabin and approach it from the upstream side.

At dawn they set out to follow an Indian trap-line trail which would take them off the Rat, as they were afraid there were too many places Johnson could ambush them in the tangle of willows and brush along the river.

The posse tramped all day. When it came time to make camp, Charley Rat assured them that they were only a few miles above Johnson's cabin. However, the next day they found that they were seven or eight miles above Johnson's camp. By the time the posse had reoriented itself near their Longstick River starting point, they had travelled twenty-eight miles in two days and had used up most of their supplies. This was going to have a strong bearing on later developments.

In the meantime, Gardlund and Lang had been detached to make a quick scout of Johnson's location by going directly down river. While circling his cabin, they noticed that smoke still poured from the chimney and they figured the trapper was still there.

The two men reported back to Eames and the inspector set up camp close to Johnson's cabin. The next morning the posse advanced up the river. The temperature hovered at forty-five below zero, a point where supplies take on overwhelming importance for sustaining a party of men and dogs in the bush. As the men approached the lonely refuge of Albert Johnson, they wondered if he would still be there. Surprisingly enough, Johnson had not moved. It was shortly before noon, January 9, 1932.

Eames and his men moved up to the river bank, which extended in a half-circle around the trapper's cabin. He shouted for Johnson to come out, explaining that King was still alive. At least Johnson would not be up for a murder

18

charge. Only ominous silence greeted Eames's confrontation. In fact, during the entire length of his defiance of the police, Johnson was never heard to say a word.

Inspector Eames then supervised a series of sorties against Johnson. All manner of ruses and diversions were used to gain access to the cabin, but the men came under such heavy fire that it was impossible to persist in the attack long enough to batter down the small four-foot door of the structure. Johnson appeared to have punched loopholes on all sides of his cabin, but somewhat confusing was the level of fire coming from them. Muzzle blasts showed that Johnson was either lying prone on the dirt floor of the cabin or was standing or kneeling in a pit.

During one sortie by Gardlund and Lang, Lang slammed the butt of his rifle against the door, jarring it open. At this point, Lang reported that Johnson was shooting from a pit. He also noted that Johnson was firing "two hand guns". These later proved to be a sawed-off shotgun and a .22 rifle with the stock sawed off.

As the hours went by, the cold began to register a telling effect on the posse. At forty-five below zero, a man has to keep moving to stay warm, but in order for the men to keep watch on the trapper's cabin they had to remain posted along the sides of the river bank. The longer a man stays outside at such low temperatures, the more food he needs to replace the body heat which is lost. Consequently, his system works overtime to keep his body at a 98-degree temperature.

Inspector Eames was well aware that the two days he lost circling the cabin now loomed increasingly in importance, as he had only two days' supply of dog food left and supplies for his men were running low. He knew that he would have to break through Johnson's defences soon or retreat for more supplies.

Fires were ordered built for the men to take turns getting warm. Here the men of the posse congregated briefly and discussed the incongruities of the desperate individual they faced. They asked each other why he had shot King, why he did not try to escape after the shooting, and who he was; but none of these questions was ever satisfactorily answered.

In January, darkness comes early at this location above the Arctic Circle (67°40′ north latitude). The siege had begun near noon and now it was nine p.m. and quite dark. Eames ordered flares to be lit, figuring the glare of the flares might blind Johnson. He also ordered the dynamite thawed out. Thawing out dynamite is a tricky process, as once the explosive is frozen, it must be handled delicately because of crystallization. Finally, this tedious task was accomplished successfully and Eames commenced throwing the dynamite sticks at the cabin in hopes of dislodging some of the logs, the door, or the roof of this seemingly impenetrable structure. The dynamite sticks were ineffective.

The men continued their raids, but hour after hour the stubborn Johnson held out against the determined efforts of the nine-man posse. The temperature dipped even lower. Something drastic would have to be done as the men of the posse could be outwaited by the man in the cabin. Johnson was fighting off the police party from the relative comfort of a heated cabin. The posse, on the other hand, was exposed to the cold.

Midnight came. The flares had long since gone out. Knut Lang volunteered to propel his lanky six-foot four-inch frame over the bank and to throw dynamite onto the roof of the cabin. Under cover of enfilading fire he carried this off successfully. The resulting explosion blew a hole in the roof and knocked off the smokestack. Lang found himself looking at Johnson, but for some unexplained reason he froze and failed to shoot him. Johnson recovered quickly, and when the smoke cleared, continued firing undeterred by the blast. Lang retreated back to the river bank.

It was near to three in the morning on January 10, 1932, when Inspector Eames decided on one last effort to dislodge Johnson from his redoubt. Eames bound up the remaining sticks of dynamite—four pounds in all—and heaved the deadly bundle across the twenty-yard clearing. The resulting blast ripped the roof off the cabin and partially caved in its sides. In hopes of gaining access to the cabin if Johnson was dazed by the blast, Karl Gardlund and Inspector Eames charged across the clearing. Gardlund carried a flashlight with him which he hoped to use in temporarily blinding Johnson. When he reached the cabin, he held the light at arm's length and shone it through the wrecked door of the cabin. However, to the surprise of Gardlund and Eames, the besieged woodsman was not only alert, but shot the flashlight out of Gardlund's hand. This attack failing, Eames and Gardlund retreated to the safety of the river bank.

Although some members of the posse suggested burning out the trapper, Eames wanted to take him alive. He then decided to go back to Aklavik. At four a.m., the force of nine men left the scene of one of the most unusual battles fought in the history of the North American frontier. One tough man had defied nine others for fifteen hours, and was still at large.

On January 14, 1932, Const. Millen and Karl Gardlund were sent back to Rat River to keep an eye on Johnson. They found that Johnson had abandoned his cabin and escaped.

In the meantime, word had been flashed over "UZK" by long-wave broadcasts to the outside world that Johnson was still holding out. First news of the initial shooting of King had been released on January 6. Somewhere along the line the label "Mad Trapper of Rat River" had been tagged on Johnson and it stuck. The fact that Johnson had held out against a larger force tended to develop the public's sympathy towards him.

This north country drama is generally credited with boosting radio from a curiosity piece to a place of importance in the news media field. For days on end the listening public remained with their ears glued to their radios, and, as a consequence of this interest, radio sales boomed throughout North America. Listeners had a field day second-guessing the case. Newspapers featured the story in headline after headline as the series of gun-fights unfolded in the grim arctic night. One newspaper came out with a front-page picture of Albert Johnson. It turned out that the photo was of an Albert Johnson, but the wrong one. Johnson of the photo walked into the newspaper office and demanded a retraction. He had been in the Northwest Territories trapping, but he was not the man the police were now chasing, and he was decidedly "not mad"!

Gardlund and Millen went through the wreckage of the "Mad Trapper's" cabin and found it hard to believe that their adversary had survived the last dynamite blast. They scoured the area in an effort to find a clue to Johnson's identity, but found nothing other than a carefully concealed stage cache suspended among some trees with no articles which could be identifying. They also found the canoe which he had purchased during the summer.

They looked for his trail, but a heavy snow which had begun during the night of the siege and continued all the next day had obliterated Johnson's tracks. At that time of the year there was only a brief period of daylight, meaning a limited period of visibility. Since they had no idea of the direction Johnson had taken, many men would have to spread out and search a one-hundred-square-mile area from the Richardson Mountains on the Yukon border to the Mackenzie River on the east.

It was obvious that Albert Johnson was no man to be taken lightly. Eames wrote in his official report: "I note in press reports that Johnson is referred to as the 'demented trapper'. On the contrary, he showed himself to be an extremely shrewd and resolute man, capable of quick thought and action, a tough and desperate character."

Eames lost one of his best men when Const. McDowell injured and re-injured his knee on his first and second trips to Johnson's cabin. Inspector Eames broadcast an appeal for volunteers over the radio and obtained the services of white and Indian trappers and two men from the Royal Canadian Signals.

On January 16, 1932, the second posse left Aklavik. The men making up this party were: John Parsons, an ex-member of the R.C.M.P.; Frank Carmichael, a trapper in the district; Noel Verville, one of three brothers who also trapped on the lower Mackenzie; Ernest Sutherland and Special Const. Lazarus Sittichinli, who were already veterans of the "war" with Johnson; and the two men from Signals, Staff Sgt. Earl F. Hersey and Quartermaster Sgt. R. F. Riddell.

Riddell was one of the north country's great bush men. He was a bridge between the old and the new in that he could take care of anything required in the way of engines yet also was an expert on mushing dogs and northern survival. Before departing, Riddell constructed several ingenious beer-bottle bombs, and made several more bombs out of old outboard engine cylinders in case Johnson barricaded himself in another cabin.

Staff Sgt. Hersey was another valuable asset to the posse. He was a former Olympic runner, and a good northern traveller.

The two men realized they could be of invaluable assistance if they could take a radio with them to relay messages to Sgt. I. Neary, who would run the radio "station" in their absence. They obtained a low-power transmitter using one 108-volt battery and 201 B tube, and a receiver to use the same battery. Their principal problem was to secure the unwieldy equipment well enough on a dog sled that the entire rig would not fall apart when they went over the first dip in the trail.

The new posse ran into the same blizzard which had

held up Millen and Gardlund and covered Johnson's tracks. Finally they made it to Rat River and set up a base camp nine miles east of Johnson's cabin. Eleven Loucheux Indians joined in the search but they, too, failed to turn up any sign of the fugitive. By January 21, Eames again faced the problem of diminishing supplies. He could maintain the large posse for four days, or cut it to a bare minimum to continue the search for ten days. He chose the latter course and selected Const. Millen to lead the search accompanied by Karl Gardlund, Noel Verville, and Sgt. Riddell.

Edgar Millen was born in Belfast, Ireland, in 1901. He attended military school as a youth, immigrated to Alberta with his parents, and eventually joined the Royal North West Mounted Police in 1920. True to his adventurous spirit, Millen volunteered for northern service and was first posted to Aklavik in 1923. From 1923 to 1931, he remained in the north country, though occasionally he visited his family in Edmonton. Millen was a popular man in the Mackenzie Delta. He was fair in his dealings with the local people and mingled with them easily. Paul Nieman, who trapped along the Arctic Red River valley before moving west to the Bell River in the Yukon Territory, said Millen had two great talents which did not hurt him any in the Arctic. One was his ability as a pastry cook, and the other was the fact that he was the best step dancer in the north country.

Millen and his party were now faced with the dilemma of choosing a direction in which to search for the trapper. The Rat River valley and its tributaries were nothing short of a jungle of cottonwood, willow, poplar, and spruce. Windfalls caused by summer squalls and winter storms served to make the tangle even worse. It was difficult enough trying to find men who became lost unintentionally without having to find a man who was avoiding them by design.

All that Millen and his men could do was to surmise what they might have done had they been in Johnson's position. They decided to continue up the Rat River. Though they had dogs, it was a slow process. The difficulties of low temperatures, drifting snow, and short days made the task of finding Johnson's trail incredibly tough. The man had the entire vast wilderness to run in, and there was always the possibility that one day he might not run, choosing rather to ambush his trackers.

The four-man party patiently worked its way up the Rat River. They combed the timber from one side of the valley to the other. From dawn to dark they scanned the snow for any telltale sign which would enable them to pick up the trail of the fugitive trapper. During this time they discovered two caches. One was loaded with half a ton of food, which they left for bait, hoping the trapper would come to it. They lay for hours in the piercing cold watching the cache through field glasses, but like a sly old wolverine, Albert Johnson did not fall for the inducement and avoided the trap.

On January 28 the temperature hit forty-seven below zero. The trackers had put in another frustrating day searching in vain for Johnson's trail. Each one of the men could run thirty miles a day behind a dog sled without getting tired. They were trail-hardened men used to long hours cutting wood, breaking trail, stabilizing a heavy supply-laden toboggan, chopping ice for water, breaking up dog fights, and other tasks in temperatures where every movement was an effort. But now even they were beginning to show signs of exhaustion. Their supplies were down to a little tea, hardtack, and bacon, and they were almost out of dog food. They travelled long and far that day and frost collected on the insides of their parkas and froze. They stopped to build a fire and warm up, and boiled tea on the way back to an outcamp they had established. While they were doing this, the ever-curious Riddell circled their resting place looking for a sign of Johnson. He spotted the faintest trace of a trail on glare ice and latched onto it like a bloodhound. Riddell followed the trail to the top of a ridge and suddenly lost it. However, a man with Riddell's years of experience was not easily discouraged. He knew how to track and set off in a wide circle in an attempt to pick up the trail. He found it again in a small creek, and examined it closely in the growing darkness. It was probably two days old. Riddell straightened up to snowshoe back to camp when a sharp crack behind him split the northern silence like a thunderclap. The tracker dived into a snowbank, at the same time levering a shell into the chamber of his rifle. Stoically he waited for the inevitable second shot. Then he realized that the sound was nothing more than a tree popping under the strain of the piercing cold. He shook his head silently as he pulled himself erect and walked back to tell his companions of his find.

On Friday, January 29, the temperature dipped even lower. It was forty-nine below zero when the men followed Riddell's trail of the previous evening. They managed to trail Johnson through several old camps, but finally lost him completely. However, they were getting to know his habits. Johnson never crossed a creek except on glare ice. Like a wolf, whenever possible he travelled the ridges where the snow was packed and a trail was hard to find. They noted that he often made a long zig-zag pattern where he might watch the men pursuing him from one side of the "z" as they proceeded up the other side. They noted that Johnson's stamina seemed to be almost superhuman. The trapper was travelling two miles to every one stepped off by his pursuers, and he was toting a heavy pack. To avoid detection in the extreme cold, he could only build fires under cover of a snowbank. He had to take time out to snare squirrels and rabbits for food as rifle shots for bigger game would give away his position. He spent long, arduous hours climbing cliffs, trotting on his snowshoes through spruce forests, and crawling among seemingly impenetrable clusters of willows and buck brush. He expertly travelled such a pattern of trails that at one point two of the trackers met head on.

The searchers now found themselves far up the Rat River. They were conferring on which way to turn when an Indian came mushing up river to tell them he had heard a shot from the vicinity of the Bear River, the point where Millen and his men had first picked up Johnson's trail. There was a distinct possibility that Johnson might have taken a chance on shooting a caribou to replenish his food supply, figuring that his trackers had lost the trail and the shot could not be heard. Millen was quite aware that anyone could have fired the shot, but though it was a slim lead, he decided to follow it up anyway. The men retraced their trail to the Bear River. Here, by continued circling they picked up the trapper's tracks again and followed them out of the Bear, down the Rat River, and five miles up a small creek which empties into the Rat River about a mile northwest of the confluence of the Rat and the Barrier rivers. In trailing him, they found odd quarters of caribou, confirming the Indian's report. They climbed a ridge running parallel to the creek but shortly thereafter lost Johnson's trail again. Then one of the men looked down into a steep canyon below them and spotted a wisp of smoke. It marked Johnson's camp.

The searchers followed the ridge until they were almost above his camp. They could see the edge of a tarp and a fire but they could not see Johnson, though they could hear him puttering and whistling among the trees. The trackers waited for two hours in the cold for a chance to get the drop on the fugitive trapper, but they never did actually see him. Waiting so long in the chill of minus fifty degrees took its toll. Frost again collected inside the men's fur clothing and at dusk they headed back to their outcamp.

In the meantime, Staff Sgt. Hersey had set out from Aklavik with a native to carry supplies to Millen and his party. Hersey arrived at their outcamp on the afternoon of Saturday, January 30, after travelling over a hundred miles, but he missed the trackers as they had already departed for Johnson's camp.

The temperature was thirty-six below and a blizzard was raging when the four trackers set out directly across the hills to apprehend Johnson. They arrived at the canyon unnoticed by the trapper. Riddell and Gardlund descended into the canyon and managed to take up positions only fifteen yards from Johnson without his seeing them. Consequently, Johnson was hemmed in against a steep cliff. Verville and Millen then started down the ridge to the creek bed. However, one of them slipped, making enough noise for Johnson to come alert and rack a shell into the breech of his rifle. He spotted Millen moving and his 30-30 Savage barked in the arctic air. Millen and Verville dropped to the ground and returned fire. Johnson evidently saw a better place to settle, jumped across his campfire, and flung himself behind an overturned tree. Karl Gardlund, a veteran of the Swedish army, was ready for him and shot at him as he leaped across the fire. He thought he hit the fugitive because Johnson seemed to collapse in a heap behind the overturned tree.

At this point Millen yelled for Johnson to give up but failed to get an answer. The four men did not dare approach the spot where Johnson had fallen immediately, so they waited to see if there was any sign that the trapper was disabled.

Minutes went by and there was no sign that the "Mad Trapper" might be still alive. It seemed like hours in the penetrating cold. An hour went by. No sound came from Johnson's direction. Silence descended on the dramatic scene being played near the top of the world. The four trackers realized there was no room for mistakes with a man as dangerous as Johnson. All of the men were as tough as the country in which they chose to live, yet they were now aware that they had run into a man who was tougher than they. Not only was he a man capable of great feats of endurance, but he was also crafty almost beyond belief. In fact, his senses were so acute and his ability to defend himself so apparent—even in the face of blasts of dynamite—the men were led to believe that Johnson might have had special training and experience, possibly police and military, at some point in his life. And since his age was estimated to be between thirty-five and forty, he might well have seen service in the First World War.

Thus, the men waited; but if they thought they could outwait a man of Johnson's capability and woodsmanship, they were to be sadly disillusioned.

After two hours had gone by "Spike" Millen decided to break the stalemate. Darkness was approaching, and if someone did not go in and rout Johnson out of his place of refuge, he more than likely would make good another getaway, if he was still alive. Millen elected to go in after the trapper, though he did so against veteran trapper Noel Verville's advice. "Git down, Spike," advised Verville, "git down or he'll kill you." Riddell joined Millen and they moved in toward Johnson's hiding place, while Verville and Gardlund covered him. They had walked about five paces when Riddell suddenly shouted "Watch it!" and ran and dived headlong over a nearby embankment just as a shot thundered and a rifle slug whistled through the trees above his head. The echo of the blast of the rifle in the severe cold resounded through the canyon as if a case of dynamite had been set off. Millen, who was parallel to and slightly behind Riddell, spotted the movement of the fugitive trapper's rifle barrel, dropped to one knee, and snapped off a shot. The noise of his high-powered rifle echoed loudly through the canyon in the depressing cold. Johnson replied in kind with his Savage. Both men missed. Millen fired again with the trapper returning two shots so quickly that the rifle blasts seemed to come as one quick burst. Millen suddenly rose up, whirled, and fell face down into the snow, his rifle falling beside him. He did not move. Karl Gardlund crawled to the fallen man and, under covering fire from his companions, tied the man's legs together with laces from his mukluks and dragged him out of Johnson's line of fire. A quick examination showed that Millen had been killed by a shot through the heart.

The three remaining trackers decided to send Sgt. Riddell back to Aklavik with the news. Gardlund and Verville built a stage cache to keep Millen's body out of reach of predators and then retired to a campsite they had established a mile away. Sgt. Earl Hersey was waiting for them with the supplies. The next morning Hersey retrieved Millen's body. At the same time, the men found that Johnson had made good his escape by climbing the vertical cliff located behind him. To do this, he had chopped hand-holds in the snow and ice with his axe and on reaching the top of the cliff had cascaded snow over his escape route in an effort to hide his trail. The men seemed to be fighting a demon rather than a human being, and the demon had won again.

The searchers looked over the scene of the third shoot-out with Johnson, and noted that when he jumped across his campfire he had settled into a hole created by a fallen spruce and was in an almost invulnerable location. The ground cavity was on an incline which extended upwards some fifteen to twenty feet higher than the searchers except for Verville in his last position. This afforded Johnson an advantage which he did not fail to utilize.

Sgt. Riddell arrived at Aklavik at noon on January 31, and reported Millen's death to Inspector Eames. Inspector Eames realized that when the news of Millen's death reached the outside world the news media would have another field day in second-guessing the case, making the search look more like a three-ring circus than the difficult task it was.

Three

Across the Mountains

THE LONGER Johnson avoided capture, the greater was the feeling for him on the part of the public, hoping the underdog might win out and escape altogether. Throughout North América people remained by their radio sets waiting for news about the great chase across the "roof" of the world. Each follower had his own opinion of the case. Whether he was a cab driver in New York, or a newsman in Vancouver, the mere mention of the "Mad Trapper" was enough to bring forth an extended conversation as to how the chase would turn out.

Inspector Eames knew the toughness of the man he pursued. Anyone who could travel on foot the distances Johnson had and still remain out of reach of trackers using dog teams was to be reckoned with. To Eames's credit he requested that a plane be dispatched to the north country for use in bringing in Johnson. Many people scoffed at the idea, for a plane had never before been used by the R.C.M.P. in tracking a man down. The necessary landings and take-offs would be perilous under the adverse conditions of such a manhunt. Eames, however, saw the not-so-obvious value of the plane: it could help alleviate his constant supply problem in feeding the dogs of the many teams involved in the search. Dogs are fed one two-pound fish a day. Five teams of five dogs each may consume as much as five hundred pounds of fish in ten days. The constant problem of their supply was hampering the search effort. As it turned out, the fugitive might have made good his escape if the aircraft had not been used.

Eames radioed a request for a plane to the commander of "G" Division, A. E. Acland, in Edmonton. His request was forwarded to R.C.M.P. headquarters in Ottawa, where it was expedited to the Cabinet of the Canadian government. Maj.-Gen. J. H. MacBrien, Commissioner of the R.C.M.P., and the Honourable Hugh Guthrie, Minister of Justice, debated the idea briefly, and then approved the use of a plane. Millen had been killed on Saturday, January 30, and by Wednesday morning a Bellanca monoplane had been leased from Western Canadian Airways and was ready for use in the hunt. The original plans were for C. H. "Punch" Dickins to take the plane to Fort McMurray, carrying additional policemen north with him. At that point, they were to be transferred to a Fokker piloted by W. R. "Wop" May.* Plans were changed and May piloted

*One of his toddling nieces bestowed that name on him, and it stuck.

the Bellanca to Aklavik with Const. William Carter and Jack Bowen coming along as passen rs.

On February 2, 1932, two days a..er going on the radio for a plane and volunteers, Eames set off down the well-worn trail to Rat River. In this party were veterans Riddell and Sittichinli, and three new men, ex-Const. Constant Ethier, Peter Strandberg, and Ernest Maring, Knut Lang and Frank Carmichael joined Eames as he detoured through Fort McPherson, as did August Tardiff, John Greenland, and ex-Const. Arthur Blake, owner of the trading post on the Peel River and one of the few men who had actually talked with Johnson.

On February 5, the party found that Johnson, after climbing the cliff to escape Millen's men, had disappeared in the jumbled array of creek beds and canyons which made up the watershed of the Rat and Barrier rivers. Johnson took to the hardpacked snow between the upper reaches of the creeks, enabling him to make fast time.

Wop May piloted the Bellanca monoplane into Aklavik via the Mackenzie River valley on February 5, and actively joined the search February 7. He landed near Eames's party and began ferrying supplies to the searchers near the Barrier River.

May was already a living legend in Canada. During the First World War he became a double ace, shooting down thirteen German planes. This included having played a part in decoying the German ace Baron Von Richthofen (nicknamed "The Red Baron") when fellow Canadian pilot Roy Brown shot him down. After the war, May scored a number of firsts in aviation in the north country. He shuttled across country one of two Junkers planes that were eventually used in the north's first oil rush at Norman Wells in 1921. Later, in 1929, May and Punch Dickins inaugurated the first regular mail and passenger run from Edmonton to Aklavik.

On February 8, Const. Sidney W. May (no relation to the pilot) , Special Const. John Moses, and several trappers joined the search after travelling over the Richardson Mountains from La Pierre House. May had been on patrol at the headwaters of the Porcupine River, staying the night in a little trappers' settlement on the Whitestone River. Others living at the Yukon settlement were John New-combe, trader Joe Netro, Charlie Thomas, and Paul Josie, whose daughter Edith was to become famous as a syndi-cated columnist with her homespun accounts of life in the north. Two white trappers, Willoughby and Reuben Mason, also had trap lines in the vicinity. Reuben Mason had come into the country in 1897, and had been a friend of Jack London when the author wintered in the Klondike. In several of his fictionalized accounts of the north, Lon-don used Mason's real name. Mason's brother, Willoughby, was another interesting character of the north. He told Const. May that he and a group of trappers were the first men to pilot a gas boat the length of the Mackenzie River. They accomplished this feat in 1910, and went on to trap white fox on the Blow River where it drains into the Arctic Ocean.

The Mason brothers had purchased a radio, and on the night of January 21, 1932, they heard a broadcast from station KNK in Fairbanks, Alaska, carrying news of the giant manhunt in progress east of the Richardson Moun-tains. When they told Const. Sid May the news he imme-diately left for La Pierre House, where he hired a posse to accompany him in joining Eames. He offered the men ten dollars a day. This was to cause Inspector Eames some consternation because all the men over the Richardson Mountains who were not with the federal government were volunteers without pay.

Sid May's party journeyed to the Barrier River base camp by way of the famous Hudson Bay portage which went up the Bell River, across Loon Lake, and down the Rat River.

At this point in the search the trackers had no idea where Johnson was heading. Some thought he might try for Alaska, but no one could be sure. Radio communications were in their infancy. Const. May later postulated that Johnson could have gone straight across the Mountains after shooting Millen, purchased supplies and dogs at La Pierre House, and then gone down the Porcupine River, and no one would have been the wiser. "As best I can remember," said May, "no one had a radio between the scene of the shooting and Fort Yukon, Alaska, which he could easily have bypassed. Once on the lower Yukon River he probably could have mingled with the many woodcutters, trappers, and prospectors and made good his escape."

Unfortunately for Johnson, he could not be sure who had a radio and who did not, with the result that he elected to avoid all men. Ultimately, he decided to make his bid for freedom by crossing the Richardson Mountains and heading westward. Sgt. Hersey, who possessed one of the fastest dog teams, and a fine lead dog by the name of Silver, later expounded on the conditions of the chase. He said that one of the determining factors in Johnson's bid to the west was the deeper snow found on the western side of the mountains. There, the snow did not tend to pack as it did on the eastern side. This would slow down a dog team, giving a man on snowshoes a better chance of escaping.

The manhunt now reached over the entire breadth of the northland. Orders went out from Edmonton for patrols to leave Whitehorse, Y.T., and to head northeast to Ross River to meet a patrol sent out from Fort Norman, N.W.T., some five hundred miles away. Patrols and airplanes were dispatched from Dawson City and Mayo in the Yukon Territory, as well as along the length of the Mackenzie River from Aklavik to Fort Simpson. Too much was now at stake for the Mounties, who were known for their dogged perseverance in bringing men to justice, to let Johnson slip away from them. The overwhelming publicity of the chase had served to put the reputation of the force on the line.

Inspector Eames ordered Const. May, Frank Jackson, who operated the trading post at La Pierre House, James Hogg, and Special Const. John Moses to mush to the headwaters of the Barrier River to look for signs of Johnson. Others scanned the Shute and Rat River passes—the most travelled routes to La Pierre House. The former was a foot-and dog-sled trail, and the latter a canoe trail in summer and a dog trail in winter. The passes had seen the footprints of many of the famous men of the north, such men as Jack McQuesten, Al Mayo, Charles Camsell, Bishop Stringer, Robert Campbell, Amos Burg, and Vilhjalmur Stefansson.

The first break in the case in over a week came on February 12 when Indian trapper Pete Alexie mushed through Rat Pass with a message from Harry Anthony at La Pierre House. Anthony said that several Indians had spotted strange snowshoe tracks east of La Pierre House. May, who had returned from the headwaters of the Barrier River, immediately raced his team to the base camp at the mouth of the Rat River. Here he found Eames, Carter, Riddell, Gardlund, and Wop May with the Bellanca. Wop May then flew the four men to Aklavik for more supplies while Const. May returned to the Barrier River Camp. The airplane was proving its utility.

Until Captain May brought the airplane into the search, Johnson had been holding his own against the trackers. Now, however, the flying machine brought the source of supplies at Aklavik and Fort McPherson to within twenty-four minutes of the men in the field. Where formerly it had taken three days to run supply sleds between Aklavik and the Barrier and Rat rivers, now it was only a matter of minutes. On February 8, 1932, May ferried over seven hundred pounds of supplies to Inspector Eames. May was absolutely fearless as a pilot. In one case, heavy snow prevented him from getting a good start on the take-off. May calmly solved this problem by telling the searchers to tie the plane to a tree and to cut the rope when he gave the signal. He accelerated the engine; the tautened rope was cut. The plane cut a swath through the snow and threatened to bog down, but at the last minute May brought it into the air, seemingly lifting it off the ground with his own body-English.

Indefatigable, May ferried supplies and constantly looked for Johnson's trail from the air. He picked up Sgt. Riddell, and in the space of a few hours they were able to trace Johnson's trail up the Barrier River, thus saving the men on foot much time and energy following blind leads which Johnson had craftily and persistently set up. For a week Johnson had been working his way up the Barrier River. On February 8, Riddell and Wop May spotted a dim trail from the air near the headwaters of the Barrier River. At this point, a stretch of the river runs parallel to the Richardson Mountains just after emerging from them. Riddell and May soon discerned that Johnson had several times turned off the river in a westerly direction as he walked upstream. He had climbed the foothills of the Richardsons and then circled back north to come out again on his old trail. Johnson apparently had hoped to circle behind the search party to visit old food caches, but had not made his circles wide enough. He kept coming back into his old trail in front of his pursuers instead of behind them.

Johnson had been living off the land for thirty days when Wop May joined the search with his Bellanca. He had escaped during a blizzard, and several more blizzards had swept the area since that time. The temperature rested between thirty and forty-five degrees below zero during much of the time Johnson was pursued, yet he was still at large.

Just how great a feat was this? Paul Nieman, who was trapping on the Bell River only half a day's journey from the Eagle River location when Johnson was eventually killed, said in a recent interview in Whitehorse: "They were all a pretty rugged bunch trailing Johnson, and for Johnson to have constantly outfought and outrun them while travelling on foot and living off the land for thirty-eight days was pretty incredible. It is rough enough just staying alive under those conditions, let alone having to be on the run."

The obstacles which Johnson would have had to overcome were many. Breaking trail with snowshoes in the areas where there was deep snow was at best an excruciating task. The physical effort of trying to escape under such conditions would make a man sweat, and the dampness thus produced would necessitate drying out his clothes. If a man is damp in his sleeping bag, he will get cold; he does not get the sleep he needs and fatigue sets in. A man who is cold needs the energy provided by food to give him heat, yet Johnson dared not use a rifle to obtain food for fear that the posse would hear the shots. He resorted to setting snares, which is a slow process for obtaining nutrition and Johnson was starving. Worst of all, he could not build a large fire, for if he did, that too would attract the eyes of the posse. Everything worked against the man, yet after thirty days he still eluded his pursuers, and his greatest feat of endurance was yet to come.

February 9 had seen a blizzard rip through the Rat and Barrier River watersheds. The blizzard swept the entire Mackenzie Delta, grounding the plane and bringing patrols to a standstill. Yet during this snowstorm, the "Mad Trapper" chose to bolt across the high ridges of the Richardson Mountains in his bid for freedom.

Outside of the few passes in the area, the Richardson Mountains represent a formidable obstacle for man or beast. They are an extension of the Rockies, and at that far northern latitude consist of barren, windswept crags, and precipices. Storms continually rake the mountains and wind-chill factors reaching the hundred-below-zero mark are common.

Local Indians said that the trapper would never try to go straight across the mountains in winter. The white trappers and veterans of the north country agreed with them. No man could cross those mountains after being chased for thirty days. The men watched the passes and Johnson was not seen, yet on February 12 Peter Alexie brought the message that Johnson was on the other side of the Richardson peaks and still going strong. To this day, no one knows how he managed an achievement which seasoned mountaineers with the best of food and equipment would have hesitated to attempt. It was a prodigious feat of endurance and only underlined what Sgt. Hersey later said of the man: "Johnson had tremendous physical ability —this was his outstanding asset."

After Johnson went over the mountains, he followed a small creek to the Bell River, cutting southwest to avoid La Pierre House. In doing this he shortcut a bend in the Bell and started heading southward along the Eagle River, which flows into the Bell.

Four

Final Shoot-Out

ON FEBRUARY 13, Eames, Carter, Gardlund, and Riddell flew to La Pierre House from Aklavik. At the same time, Constable Sid May, Special Constables John Moses and Lazarus Sittichinli, Signals Staff Sgt. Hersey, Joseph Verville (brother of Noel), Constant Ethier, Frank Jackson, and Peter Alexie, started across the mountains through Rat Pass.

The airborne party landed at La Pierre House about

noon. May set out immediately in the Bellanca to look for Johnson's trail, and in a short time found it leading up the Eagle River from the Bell. Here Johnson's tracks disappeared among the many trails of a herd of caribou. Johnson, always wily, had obviously decided the best chance to hide his trail was by following the caribou as long as they were headed away from his pursuers.

On Sunday, February 14, flying conditions were poor and Wop May was able to get in only an hour's flying time. However, it was enough to pick up Johnson's trail twenty miles up the Eagle River from its confluence with the Bell.

By February 15, the party which had undertaken the trip through the pass arrived at La Pierre House. That same day fog closed in, forcing the plane to stay on the ground, but the dog-sled party from across the mountains, after a short break, set out to follow Eames, Gardlund, Carter, and Riddell, who had left on foot to follow Johnson earlier in the day. Within a few hours the two parties were united and proceeded together up the Eagle River.

The Eagle River winds like a snake through a country of low-rolling hills and little timber. The trackers cut across numerous bends to save time. In order to show Wop May where they were when visibility became good enough for him to fly, the men cut spruce trees and formed arrows in the snow pointing out their way.

On February 16 the fog was still bad. The Bellanca was grounded as the searchers continued up the Eagle River. News of the progress of the manhunt radiated down the Porcupine River valley to Old Crow. Neil Macdonald recalls that the men of Old Crow were busy forming another posse to stop Johnson if he went down the Porcupine. But an elderly woman shaman of the Old Crow band told them, "You no go look. One sleep and he die."

The sky was gradually clearing when the posse started out on the morning of February 17. As it turned out, they were on one of the many hairpin turns in the river, the trackers having camped on one side of the "pin" and Albert Johnson on the other. The posse made considerably more noise than usual because the snow was all cut up by caribou tracks.

Johnson probably heard this from his side of the "pin" and thought the trackers were coming down river rather than going up. In addition (as Sid May ascertained later), he had gone up river and run into ski tracks of Bill Anderson and Phil Barnstrum, partners who trapped the headwaters and middle section of the Eagle River. Fearing the ski tracks represented advance scouts of the posse (Gardlund had been using skis), he had turned around and was backtracking.

Shortly before noon the posse ran head-on into Johnson. Sgt. Hersey, with his strong team of seven Mackenzie River huskies, was in the lead. The snow was not packed, but even so the going was fairly good for that area. Said Hersey, "If the snow had been a few inches deeper, I would have had to run ahead of the team with my small trail snowshoes. In that snow area we normally carry small trail snowshoes and also large snowshoes for the deep snow. Johnson was backtracking, stepping in his old tracks, and obviously thought we were behind him. He was startled when he saw me. He put on his homemade snowshoes which I recognized, and started for the bank of the river."

Hersey grabbed his rifle and started to fire. At about the same time, Joe Verville and Sid May came up and also started firing at the trapper. Johnson ran a few steps, and then whirled and snapped off a shot at Hersey. The slug of the 30-30 Savage hit Hersey, who was in a kneeling position firing his rifle. The impact of the deadly missile lifted Hersey right off the ground and he cartwheeled into the snow. The bullet had smashed through his left elbow, ploughed through his left knee, and then ripped through his chest.

Const. Sid May, who thought Hersey had been killed by

1. Dog team and musher bringing wood into Aklavik. Even above the Arctic Circle spruce trees grow in the river valleys, but beyond them the land is barren, wind-swept tundra.

2. Constable Alfred "Buns" King on patrol near Dawson in the late 1920s.

3. Russell Creek trading post *circa* 1928. Second from left is Sam Isaac who met Arthur Nelson here when the trapper was buying supplies at the post.

4. Staff-Sergeant Earl Hersey and dog team at Aklavik in 1932.

5. Hersey, shown with the team's lead dog, Silver.

(above) 6.   Pit cabin of Johnson on Rat River after it was blown up by the Mounties during the siege of January 9, 1932.

(top right) 7.   Constable Edgar "Spike" Millen was killed by Johnson in the shoot-out of January 30, 1932.

(lower right) 8.   Mounted Policemen who figured in the case of the Mad Trapper of Rat River relaxing near Dawson City in the summer of 1927: James Purdie, Tom Coleman, "Nipper" Carcoux, and Alfred "Buns" King.

(above) 9. The Bellanca aircraft, piloted by W. R. "Wop" May during the search for Albert Johnson, loading supplies at Aklavik.

(lower left) 10. Jack Bowen, R. F. Riddell, and
W. R. "Wop" May beside the search aircraft.

(below) 11. May's plane waiting for the fog to clear at Aklavik.

12.   Don Parks and dog team in front of Robert Levac's store at Fraser Falls in the spring of 1929.

(left) 13.   Special Constable Lazarus Sittichinli was one of the leading dog mushers in the chase of Albert Johnson.

(centre) 15.   Special Constable John Moses took part in the final battle with Johnson on the Eagle River.

(right) 16.   Constable Sid May mushed from the headwaters of the Porcupine River to join the pursuit of Johnson.

14. Constable Claude Tidd on patrol up the Ross River in 1928.

18. This second photograph was taken from the plane by May during the final stages of the fight. Johnson (1) lies in the middle of the river. One man (2) has out-flanked him and may be seen immediately in front of the trees. Another (3) is shooting at Johnson from his right. Hersey (4) lies wounded in the snow. Three men (5) are sniping at Johnson from the west bank of the river in front of the tree line. Two others (6), probably Const. Sid May and Joe Verville, lie in the centre of the river. Seven bullets hit Johnson before a slug through the spinal column killed him.

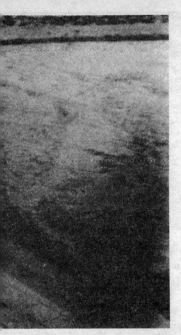

17. This photograph of the historic Eagle River shoot-out on February 17, 1932, was taken by W. R. "Wop" May from his plane. Johnson (1) knelt and fired at Earl Hersey (2), seriously wounding him. After attempting to climb the east bank, Johnson moved to the centre of the river (3), where he was killed. Hersey was carried to the east bank (4) of the river.

(left and above) 19, 20.   Death photographs of Albert Johnson.

21, 22.   Sketches of Johnson based on the death photographs.

(right) 23, 24.   This photograph, taken by Frank Slim at Ross River, Y.T., in 1927, is the only known photograph of Arthur Nelson, the fair-haired man standing on the left near the tree. An enlargement of the face is too indistinct to provide a definite link with Albert Johnson, but the sketch below is based on it and death photographs of Johnson.

25. Johnson artifacts in the Royal Canadian Mounted Police museum, in Regina, Saskatchewan. The snowshoes weighed ten pounds each.

the trapper, signalled for the party to break into two segments, and they moved up both sides of the river toward the trapper, who had by now run forty yards and thrown himself into the snow. He rolled over onto his back and eased his arms out of the pack and then used it as a bulwark. Karl Gardlund, Frank Jackson, John Moses, and Constant Ethier darted to the east bank of the river and ran north, firing as they went. Lazarus Sittichinli, Const. William Carter, Peter Alexie, and Sgt. Riddell swept up the west bank of the river also concentrating their fire on Johnson. Inspector Eames joined Const May in the centre of the river, and shouted twice for Johnson to surrender.

In the space of a few minutes, Gardlund, Jackson, Moses, and Ethier had outflanked Johnson and were located on the high bank of the river with Johnson below and between the two groups. The sniping from above shortly began to take effect. One shot hit ammunition in Johnson's pocket, and he jinked violently when it exploded and took a chunk of flesh out of his thigh. Another bullet slammed into his shoulder and still another into his side, but the trapper kept on firing.

Inspector Eames, for the third time, called on Johnson to surrender, but there was no answer other than the bark of the 30-30 Savage and a wave of his arm. The posse poured fusillades of lead into the trapper's shallow sanctuary.

Wop May and Jack Bowen had been shooting pictures of the battle from their airplane. It was so cold they could even hear the rifle shots above the roar of the engine. Said May, "We came roaring down the river and once again I peered down at Johnson in his snow trench. Then, as I circled over the posse, I saw a figure lying on a bedroll and realized that one of our party had been hit. I circled back up river, passing over the posse and Johnson. As I flew over the fugitive's lair it seemed as though he was lying in an unnatural position. Swinging back, I nosed the Bellanca down till our skis were tickling the snow. Johnson, I could plainly see as I flashed past, was lying face down in the snow, his right arm out-flung grasping his rifle. I knew as I looked that he was dead."

May rocked the wings of his plane to indicate that Johnson was dead. At about the same time, Sid May walked forward, rifle in hand, ready for anything. He hooked the rifle barrel under Johnson's body and turned him over. The "Mad Trapper" was dead; a bullet through the spine was the shot which ended his life.

Wop May landed the Bellanca and walked over to look at Johnson. "As I stooped over and saw him," said May, "I got the worst shock I've ever had. For Johnson's lips were curled back from his teeth in the most terrible sneer I've ever seen on a man's face. . . . It was the most awful grimace of hate I'd ever seen—the hard-boiled, bitter hate of a man who knows he's trapped at last and has determined to take as many enemies as he can with him down the trail he knows he's going to hit."

Wop May, Jack Bowen, and Joe Verville then loaded Hersey onto the plane. Hersey, though seriously wounded, was conscious the whole time. In an interview with the author he said, "Little time was lost in loading me into the plane. It seems that we were in Aklavik within an hour. Feeling returned to my legs and oddly enough the severe pain was in my knee. Dr. Urquhart said this was due to damage to the nerves. The doctor went through the hole in my chest and tied off the arteries which were bleeding so much. An anesthetic was not used."

However, the doctor had some more work to do, as Hersey explained. "Later, I complained of a wrinkle in the sheets. The doctor gently moved me on my side, found the bullet just under the skin, and cut it out immediately with a small knife. He was justly proud that he had not endeavoured to look for the bullet with a probe." Hersey still has the slug.

Johnson's body was taken to La Pierre House by dog sled and the next day was flown to Aklavik, where pictures were taken of him and Dr. Urquhart conducted a complete physical examination of his body. Later, he was buried in an unmarked grave. A coroner's jury comprising C. G. Matthews, I. Neary, N. E. Hancock, R. H. Kilgour, J. Parsons, and L. Scott-Brown found that "Albert Johnson came to his death from concentrated rifle fire from a party composed of members of the Royal Canadian Mounted Police and others . . ." on February 17, 1932, confirming the old woman's prediction in Old Crow that "One sleep and he die."

Ironically, Johnson's war with the police was to benefit the people of the Mackenzie Delta. The publicity caused by the chase, and the jeopardy posed by possible rifle slugs in Hersey and King, pointed up the fact that the hospital at Aklavik did not have an X-ray unit, and one was promptly supplied.

Dr. Urquhart's physical examination revealed that there were no operation scars on Johnson.* The physician stated that the trapper was five feet nine and one-half inches tall, weighed 150 pounds and had light blue eyes and light brown hair. Johnson's nose was upturned and his ears were lobed. Urquhart estimated that he was between thirty-five and forty years old. Fingerprints were taken of him and sent to Ottawa and Washington, D.C.

No one came forth to claim the body of the man, and the fingerprints drew a blank. To this day he has never been identified, though there are few individuals acquainted with the story who do not have a strong opinion about Johnson's identity.

The "Mad Trapper" has been identified as a Swede, a Russian, an American, a Dane, a Finn, a Norwegian, and a Canadian. It has been said at various times that he trav-

*There is some conjecture as to what Urquhart meant in the qualifying description of no "operation" scars.

elled into the Peel River country from Eagle, Alaska; Keno, Y.T.; Dawson City, Y.T.; or Norman Wells, N.W.T.

Versions given of Johnson's motives in shooting three men are as many as there are quirks in man's psychological makeup. Since the case in a sense belongs to the public, it has given millions of armchair detectives an opportunity to give vent to their opinions about the "Mad Trapper".

Some of the many "detectives" say the trapper was a loner suffering from nothing more than cabin fever; others are adamant in stating that he was a spy for a foreign state, possibly Russia; many are of the opinion that Johnson was wanted in the United States for bank robbery, or murder, or both. Numerous individuals are steadfast in their belief that Johnson became involved with an Indian girl and that a jealous lover "set him up" by complaining to the Mounties that Johnson was springing his traps. One prevalent story was that Johnson hated all Mounties because one once "stole" his girl. Another account reverses the situation and has him departing with a Mountie's girl. Yet another version has the trapper eternally mad at the world because his wife was raped and killed by some miners. One version has Johnson as an ex-Mountie; another, as a former provincial policeman. The opinions go on and on, and it seems certain that the true story of his motives will never be known. Albert Johnson's identity is another matter. There seems to be enough material on hand to trace him, and possibly someday his "outside" background will be established.

When Johnson was killed he had the following possessions: $2,410 in Canadian bills in denominations of $50, $20, and $10, and two U.S. $5 bills; a small glass jar containing five pearls valued at $15 and five pieces of gold dental work of four pennyweight (twenty pennyweight to a Troy ounce) valued at $3.20; another jar containing thirteen pennyweight of alluvial gold valued at $9.36; a model 99 Savage 30-30 rifle; an Iver Johnson sawed-off shotgun (16 gauge); a Winchester .22 rifle model 58; thirty-nine 30-30 shells and four 16-gauge shotgun shells; a pocket compass; packages containing a total of thirty-two pills; an axe; a packsack; lard can and lid; a dead squirrel and a dead whiskey jack.* Characteristic of the uncommunicative nature of the man was the fact that no written clues were found on his person in the form of a letter or identity card, though he may have burned these while starting campfires during the chase. It was as if he had come from nowhere, and was a "non-person".

*For a complete history of Johnson's effects see Appendix "A", Exhibit "C".

Part Two

Arthur Nelson

Five

Dease Lake

George Adsit sat in his cabin far up Thibert Creek in the Cassiar District of northern British Columbia. It was the spring of 1933. He picked up a copy of *True Detective Mysteries Magazine* which his son, Buck, had brought up that day from the trading post at Porter's Landing on Dease Lake. It was six months old. A story entitled "Trapping the Mad Trapper of Rat River" caught his eye, and he settled back in his chair reading by the light of an oil lamp. Told by pilot Wop May, the tale was a dramatic one and held Adsit's attention. The more he read about the "Mad Trapper" Albert Johnson, the more familiar the man seemed. The placer miner racked his brains trying to figure out the connection. Finally, he turned a page and saw Albert Johnson's death picture. The man was Arthur Nelson, who had trapped on Thibert Creek, and had worked for Dease Creek placer mines for a time during the 1926 season.

"Buck!" George exclaimed, calling to his son. "Look at this. That's Arthur Nelson." Though only a lad in 1926, Buck recalled Nelson. "You're right," Buck commented. "It sure enough looks like Nelson."

The senior Adsit nodded and said, "By God, Ed Asp should take a look at this." He turned to his son. "Buck, tomorrow take this picture down to Ed and see if he thinks it's Art Nelson."

Asp was a Swede who had had a speaking acquaintance-ship with Nelson, who very possibly was also Swedish.

The next day Buck Adsit showed the photo to Asp. "That's him all right," said Asp with little hesitation. "Well, what do you know! There couldn't be two guys like Arthur Nelson."

Thus arose the first indication that the man called Arthur Nelson, and "The Mad Trapper of Rat River", Albert Johnson, may have been one and the same person.*

Gold was probably the attraction which brought Nelson to Dease Lake. A gold rush started in August 1924 when prospectors William Grady and J. H. Ford discovered gold on a stream they named Goldpan Creek near the head of Dease Lake. They weren't overly impressed by the few ounces of gold they found and casually recorded their claims later in Telegraph Creek. Perhaps they were too casual, as before the day was over rumours had blown up

*For R.C.M.P. reference to Nelson in the Yukon, see *R.C.M.P. Annual Report for 1934*, King's Printer, Ottawa.

the two-and-one-half-ounce discovery into a major gold strike. Consequently, the captain and crew of the barge and boat service on the Stikine River embarked for the gold fields. If anyone wanted to go out to Wrangell, he would have to "paddle his own canoe". The crew staked a host of claims on Goldpan Creek and returned to Telegraph Creek. Any complaints which arose as a result of their bolt for the gold fields were shrugged off by the captain. Gold was gold, and nobody but the old and infirm would ignore such a calling; thus they ventured down the river to Wrangell. The crew of the boat service embellished the story of the gold and fanned the flames of the rumour even more, not unaware, of course, that a stampede in September would improve their earnings substantially before freeze-up beached them for the winter.

The rush began. Word was passed by telegraph and word of mouth and the usual aggregate of prospectors, hardrock miners, cooks, fishermen, loggers, newspapermen, and anyone else with gold fever headed for the new diggings. Goldpan Creek was located twelve miles east of the south end of Dease Lake. Since Dease Lake is drained by the Dease River, which runs from the north end of the lake, the south end is called the head of the lake. A road which had been slashed through by Captain William Moore in a previous rush to the area in 1874, and which now was more a trail than a road, connected the head of the lake with Telegraph Creek. Many of the 1924 stampeders who first reached Goldpan Creek went in this way. Others journeyed overland by way of the Teslin trail from Atlin, another gold-mining area located to the northwest of Dease Lake. Still more gold seekers hastened to Dease Lake and Goldpan Creek by way of the Liard River. This was a rugged trip which included portaging around the Rapids of the Drowned at Hell's Gate and then continuing up the Liard to the mouth of the Dease and up the Dease until the lake was reached. The lake had to be traversed, and from the head of the lake the men walked the rest of the way to Goldpan Creek. Still others drifted in by way of the Muddy (Ketchika) River, and yet more walked up the Telegraph Trail from the mining town of Stewart located at the head of Portland Canal. This route took them north past Echo and Edontennajon lakes to Dease Lake.

By the end of November 1924 over two hundred miners had come into the area. Snow had fallen and the creeks were in the process of freezing up, but, like prospectors the world over, these stampeders were undeterred by what they could not see. They staked their claims whether they saw any sign of gold or not. Then they returned to the areas from whence they had sprung, and came back in 1925 and 1926 to pursue the rainbow's elusive end. In August 1926, just as this gold rush was about to die, Arthur Nelson suddenly appeared, as if out of nowhere. No one knew exactly where he had come from when he first put in an appearance at Porter's Landing at the foot of Thibert Creek to purchase supplies. Here he met Edward Asp and his family. Asp had come into the country after working as a logger and prospector in a region stretching from Wisconsin to Montana in the United States. Before that he had been a seaman from Sweden coming to America through the port of New Orleans. Nelson told Asp that he was a trapper and that he poled a boat up the Stikine River. Both men spoke English and Swedish fluently. When they talked about trapping, Asp offered to let Nelson use the upper part of his trap line which was located on Thibert Creek. Nelson took up the offer and proceeded to hike up the creek until he came to a point about five miles above Mosquito Creek, or twenty miles up Thibert Creek from Porter's Landing.

Here he built his cabin, using neither nail nor spike. The cabin still stands today as an excellent example of what an expert craftsman can do with an axe. Every part of the cabin showed the use of either an axe or a hand drill.

Arthur Nelson was to spend one winter in this cabin. Residents recalled that Arthur Nelson had light brown hair that bleached in the summer sun. He seldom talked with anyone, and only occasionally ventured forth to areas where there were other people. This trait was not unknown among those men who sought to remain alone in the bush, but Nelson seemed to have a certain inner hostility about him which made some people he met feel uncomfortable. Even if Nelson had not been a quiet, withdrawn man, his eyes would still have been a source of comment. Half-closed, in a seemingly perpetual squint, they were light blue, almost grey—the colour of cold steel, radiating a certain chilling indifference which startled those who did not know him well. Those who knew him personally did not dislike him, however. They decided he was just by nature very quiet.

Thibert Creek was one of the better gold-bearing creeks of the region. It had been discovered in 1872 by Henry Thibert, a Minnesota American of French descent. He and a Scotsman by the name of McCullough had set off from the Red River of the prairies in 1871 and travelled via the Mackenzie River and the Liard River as far as the abandoned Hudson's Bay post at Fort Halkett. This was located in close proximity to where Liard Hot Springs is found today near the Alaska Highway. Here the two men found gold at a point on the river which later became known as McCullough's Bar. The two prospectors passed the winter at the abandoned post and then proceeded up the Liard to Dease Lake, where they hoped to catch a good supply of fish to stock their larder for the operation on the Liard. However, Indians living at the lake informed them of a gold strike where many white men were working on the Stikine at a location called Buck's Bar. Being typical prospectors, with a bird in the bush being worth two in the hand, the two men abandoned the idea of returning to their own discovery. They left their boats at the head of Dease Lake and walked south to the discovery of the Stikine. To their chagrin, they found all the profitable ground occupied by the time they got there. Others in the same predicament joined them and Thibert and McCullough turned right around and journeyed back to Dease Lake. From here they hoped to get back to their original discovery. While snow-shoeing up the Stikine, McCullough went through the ice, and though rescued, died later as a result of exposure. The rest of the party arrived back at Dease in the spring of 1873 only to find that Thibert's boats had been stolen. Being a philosophical sort of breed, the prospectors decided to walk down the west side of Dease Lake and prospect as they went along. The gold seekers were thus occupied when they found gold on a bench three miles up the creek which they named after Thibert. Thibert and his party worked the creek throughout the summer of 1873. It did not take long before "flies" were attracted to the "honey" and a dozen more prospectors and placer miners joined the group already on the creek. An overflow of the discovery resulted in the sons of Captain William Moore, Bernard and young William, discovering gold on Dease Creek while their father worked on Thibert Creek. This attracted even more miners and resulted in the gold rush of 1874 to Dease Creek and the entire area, which was designated the Cassiar. However, production gradually fell off and was virtually nonexistent until the stampede of 1924, when Thibert and other creeks came alive again with stakers, and it was on the fringes of this rush that Nelson built his cabin on Thibert Creek.

The inhabitants of Thibert Creek and its tributaries were a typical cross-section of the men to be found seeking gold along any creek in the north country. Immediately upstream from Nelson's cabin was the tributary of Vowel Creek, upon which an old-timer in the area, Phil Hankin, and Captain Scotti, an itinerant prospector, teamed up to sluice a small amount of gold. Hankin was a wonderful raconteur of stories of the north country. He had worked for years on the Telegraph Trail as a telegrapher, and there were few people in the country whom he did not know. Hankin was to remain in the Dease Lake region until he took his own life with a 30-30 rifle in his cabin on Cottonwood Creek shortly after the end of the Second World War. He was suffering from cancer, and in the way of many an old-timer, thought it was better to use the rifle than to suffer the double agony of a prolonged illness and confinement in a hospital bed.

George Adsit was located on the downstream side of Nelson's cabin. Adsit had come into the country in 1898 while he was working as a cowboy driving cattle up the Rocky Mountain trench, a huge valley which runs from Prince George, B.C., to Watson Lake, Y.T. He was a tough holdover from the wild American west. He is said to have been a friend of Charlie Russell, the famous Montana cowboy artist who was to get as much as $30,000 a painting before he died. Adsit also was an acquaintance of Granville Stuart, head of a group of vigilantes who hanged a number of cattle rustlers in Montana, and of Charlie Siringo, the famous cowboy detective. Often, when he recounted stories about the old days, listeners wondered just which side of the law George was on when he met such men as Siringo and Stuart. There are rumours which still persist connecting George Adsit with Butch Cassidy's Hole-in-the-Wall gang. And going by Adsit's ability with a .45 revolver, these rumours tend to take on a degree of credibility.

George Edzerza, retired big game guide who once lived in Telegraph Creek, went on many a hunt with the old cowboy. He said that Adsit seldom missed downing birds on the wing with his pearl-handled .45 revolvers, and was the "best pistol shot I've ever seen"—and Edzerza has seen a host of men firing sidearms in his day.

George Adsit's facility with a .45 was to cause him

trouble later on. Several years after the stampede of 1924, Adsit leased his property on Mosquito Creek, which empties into Thibert Creek five miles below Nelson's cabin, to J. R. Gibson and J. H. Searfoss of Seattle. As part of the agreement, George was to be informed each time the two men were to sluice gravels which had been stockpiled for the purpose of "cleaning up" the gold. It is quite natural in such cases for the lessor to want to be on hand when the lessee extracts the gold. If the lessor is not on hand, there is occasionally a tendency on the part of the lessee to take more than he is supposed to under the agreement. At any rate, whether Gibson and Searfoss were guilty of an infraction of the agreement is now immaterial. George Adsit thought they were guilty and that was enough. He stormed down to the claim with his .45's and insisted that the two men leave his property. When they balked, he fired several shots around their feet to hasten them along. Under ordinary circumstances, this was alarming enough, but the aging Adsit suffered from palsy, a disease which affected his muscles and caused him to shake. Searfoss and Gibson complained to the police of the incident and Adsit was called into court in Telegraph Creek. His conversation with the judge went something like this:

"Did you mean to shoot them?"

"No, just scare them."

"With your shaking wouldn't you be afraid of hitting them?"

"No, I shoot between shakes."

This was the same Adsit, along with his son, Buck, who later figured prominently in identifying Albert Johnson as Arthur Nelson.

There were other men working on Thibert Creek in 1926. Below Adsit's operation, George Ball and George Finn were doing their best to abstract gold from Deloire Creek, a tributary of Thibert Creek.

George Ball had been in the country for years building

up a ranch on the Stikine River. Ball's ranch had been the landing field for four U.S. Army planes which made the first flight into the north country on their way to Alaska in August 1920. Ball had prospected over much of the country of northern British Columbia and the southwestern part of the Northwest Territories, being one of the first individuals to see the utility of a plane and to hire one for the purpose of prospecting in inaccessible regions. One of the areas in which Ball prospected was the Nahanni River and its tributaries. This area is known for its allure for gold seekers. It is also known for the number of disappearances and deaths which have occurred under mysterious circumstances. Men keep going back to the Nahanni seemingly to take up the challenge where others have failed. Ball was one of the many from Dease Lake to heed the call of the Nahanni and the lure of lost gold.

Of such kind were the men, Nelson among them, who cast their lot with the alluring north.

In the late summer of 1926, Nelson went to work for Dease Creek Mines under the management of J. B. Blick. Dease Creek Mines and the Dickinson Mining Company had been incorporated in Seattle in 1923. Both companies commenced aggressive exploration programs on Dease Creek in 1924. The need for planks in building flumes, cabins, and sheds resulted in the construction of a sawmill by Dease Creek Mines eight miles above Laketon, the small settlement at the mouth of Dease Creek. A road was built to the property.

Nelson worked on the monitor for Dease Creek Mines and may have worked at the sawmill. Characteristically, Nelson seldom spoke to anyone, even when spoken to. He was a good worker, and Edward Asp later reported that no one was any better with an axe or a saw. J. B. Blick commented that for the two summers Nelson worked for his company, "He didn't say a word, and if he said anything other than 'give me an axe' or 'get out of the way' or other such verbal necessities in a day's work, I never heard it." Other than the above comments, all that Blick could remember of the man's talking was when he asked for his pay.

Arthur Nelson would occasionally engage in a poker game. This was the nearest he ever came to being social other than when he stopped to visit Asp's place at Porter's Landing. Even during games of poker he seldom said anything except what was absolutely necessary in the progress of the game. Perhaps significantly, Nelson never visited Ed Asp until his wife, Dorothy, left Porter's Landing to have a baby in Telegraph Creek in November 1926. Nelson appeared to be extraordinarily shy in the presence of women.

Seldom seen or heard, Nelson passed two years at Dease Lake. He did mention fragments of his past to Edward Asp. On one occasion he talked about logging in the Wisconsin woods, and while on the subject mentioned casually that he had been "on the Great Lakes". It may be assumed by this that he meant either as a seaman or as a fisherman. He also said that he had been a "tie-hacker" at one time, presumably meaning that he had worked for either a railroad or a sawmill sub-contractor to a railroad. He also mentioned trapping at Echo Lake on the Telegraph Trail.

Art Nelson trapped that winter between Dease Lake and Teslin Lake along the Jennings River, the old '98ers' trail to the Klondike. This was in the shadow of the mountains in which the $100 million Cassiar asbestos discovery was to be staked twenty years later.

The next summer he again worked in the placer operations but the work force on both major operations in the area was substantially reduced from the previous summers. In the beginning of August 1927 Nelson suddenly disappeared, leaving a pack hanging in a tree which contained a .38 calibre Smith and Wesson revolver. Asp, Adsit, Hankin, and others who lived along the creek respected the man's property and left the pack hanging where it was.

And though it was a bit unusual for a man to leave an area so abruptly, Nelson's neighbours were accustomed to his withdrawn ways, and judged that he would be back. He never returned.

Six

Teslin, Ross River, and the Lost McHenry Gold Mine

ONE DAY IN mid-August 1927, Andy Bride, trading-post manager for Taylor and Drury at Teslin, Yukon Territory, looked up from his chores and saw a smudge fire built across an arm of Teslin Lake. Signalling by smudge was a generally accepted method of obtaining transportation across the stretch of the lake now spanned by a bridge on the Alaska Highway. A lone figure of a man stood next to the fire. Bride went over in his boat, picked up the stranger, and gave him a ride to the north bank of the arm of the lake. Members of the Fox and Johnson families of Teslin recalled the stranger as carrying a huge pack and two bearskins for sleeping robes. Later that day the newcomer camped on the beach below Tom and Lily Smith's cabin. He accepted an invitation to have tea with them and during the course of conversation said that his name was Arthur Nelson and that he had walked the beach of Teslin Lake coming up from the south. Nelson said that the sound of machinery had attracted him toward that area. Smith explained that Albert Huston was running equipment at his mining operation on Wolf Creek. Other than saying that he had walked the beach, Nelson was non-committal about his origin or his destination. The next morning when the Smiths got up, Nelson was gone.

Several weeks later Frank Slim, Drury Magundy, Frank Jim, Paddy Smith, and Jimmie Smith were camped on the Lapie River trail sixteen miles south of Ross River post. They were in the process of staking claims for Whitehorse trader William Puckett. The Canol road now traverses the trail on which the men were camped. The prospectors were eating supper when a stranger plodded into camp. He was invited to sit down with the men, and accepted. He was very quiet, and to Frank Slim he seemed to be on the nervous side. "He was always looking around," Slim said later. The loner stayed with the Indians until he had finished eating and then he put his pack on and headed north, saying he was going to Ross River.

The Taylor and Drury trading post at Ross River, Y.T., was located at the confluence of the Ross and Pelly rivers. Roy Buttle was manager of the post for the pioneer traders Bill Drury and Ike Taylor. The two owners of the post were men of such business acumen that they successfully fended off the giant Hudson's Bay Company and competed successfully with the Northern Commercial Company for over half a century. The company still operates today under the name of Taylor and Drury, or as it is more commonly called, "T & D".

Buttle was puttering around in front of the store on August 21, 1927, when the crack of a rifle shot resounded across the Pelly River. Buttle was not unduly surprised by this; it was customary for a foot traveller to attract attention this way if he desired a ride across the river. Buttle noticed a ruggedly built, blond-haired man of average height wave across the river. He waved back and walked down to his small river boat and rowed it to the opposite bank. The stranger climbed into the boat. He was carrying a large pack, quite usual and necessary for any man backpacking across country in the Yukon in the summer.

"Nice day," Buttle said while busy at the oars of the boat.

The stranger nodded, though he did not say anything.

Buttle glanced over the stranger's shoulder and saw Frank Etzel hoeing potatoes in his garden. Frank waved and Buttle waved back. Buttle chuckled, shook his head, and then spoke again. "You can never keep a secret up here. You are here only two minutes and I bet all of Ross River already knows it." Buttle paused and added, "You know we don't get many visitors. In two years we've seen Pete Frederickson, Pete Picard, Pete Linder, Ole Bredvik, Fred Swanson, Fred Berg, Charlie Carlson, and now . . . ?"

"Art," the stranger filled in, "Art Nelson."

Buttle nodded. "Another Swede!" He smiled and said, "Why all the Swedes head for Ross River is something I can't quite figure out."

Nelson did not deny that he was Swedish. When they reached the shore Nelson climbed up the river bank and nodded to Buttle. "Thanks," he said while shouldering his pack. "I have to buy some stuff. I'll be back after I make camp."

"You can stay in a spare cabin we have here if you want," Buttle offered.

"No, I'll be back," Nelson said and walked off.

Buttle shrugged and watched the newcomer walk away. He noted that Nelson, though only around thirty-five, was stoop-shouldered, as though he had been carrying a pack all his life.

The next day Arthur Nelson returned to the trading post. He had camped about a half-mile above the community of Ross River where many of the Indians were still nomadic and lived in tents. Nelson asked Buttle the best way to get to the headwaters of the Macmillan River. Buttle told him he could go by trail or by boat, but in the latter case he would have to line or pole up the Ross River to Sheldon Lake, and from there cut across on foot to the Macmillan, a distance of about twenty miles. Nelson figured that a boat would be the best conveyance for his supplies, and decided to build the craft at the trading post after Buttle agreed to sell him some lumber. Buttle offered to give him a hand, but the silent visitor declined. Every night the stranger would walk back to his camp and then return again in the morning.

After a day or two, when Nelson noticed that Buttle was not the type to ask many questions about a man's past, he accepted his help. It took nine days to build the boat. During this time the trader learned that Nelson was originally from the United States, and had been raised on a small farm in North Dakota. He said he had trapped the winter before in the area between Teslin and Dease Lake, and had walked to Ross River by way of the Teslin–Quiet Lake–Lapie River trail. He also said he had worked in the mines at Anyox, B.C., before he went to the Dease Lake region.

Buttle detected the faintest trace of a Scandinavian accent in Nelson's speech. He also noticed that Nelson would have nothing to do with anyone in the Ross River settlement. This stranger and his distant attitude did not go unnoticed by the other residents of Ross River. Indians and whites alike commented on the unsociable character of the newcomer.

Frederick Berg, who trapped in the Pelly Lakes region

northeast of Ross River, met Nelson in 1928 when he journeyed into the trading post to purchase supplies. He did not like the man. He said Nelson seemed to have a silent arrogance about him that made him objectionable.

Joe Ladue, at that time about forty years old, noted that Nelson was not only an unsociable person, but that he never went anywhere without a rifle. Even walking the short distance into the trading post was apparently reason enough for the man to sling his rifle over his shoulder.

In late August or early September 1927, Nelson left the trading post and poled and lined up Ross River. Before leaving he told Buttle that he would probably trap somewhere around the headwaters of the Ross and the Macmillan rivers.

In 1927 Ross River was an artery for Indian and white trappers journeying from Fort Norman in the Northwest Territories to Fort Selkirk in the Yukon Territory. The trading post, originally called Nahanni Post, had been in operation since the turn of the century when it was built by traders Poole Field and Clement Lewis.

The first white man to pass by the location had been Robert Campbell in 1840. Campbell named the Pelly River for Sir Edmund Pelly, and Ross River for Duncan Ross, Chief Factor of the Hudson's Bay Company. Few white men travelled through the region for three decades following the pillaging of Fort Selkirk by Chilkat Indians in 1852. This incident caused the Hudson's Bay Company to withdraw from the region.

In 1900, Clement Lewis and Poole Field ascended Ross River to a beautiful lake they named Rudyard Lake. A prominent mountain which rises northwest of the lake they named Kipling Mountain. Both names originated from the two trappers' predilection for reading the works of the famous poet and author Rudyard Kipling. When big-game hunter Charles Sheldon discovered a new species of mountain sheep in close proximity to Kipling Mountain a few years later, the Canadian government changed the name of the lake and the mountain to Sheldon.

It was to this area that Nelson paddled his boat after lining through Prevost Canyon and Skookum Rapids, and the small lakes named after Lewis and Field. He moved into an abandoned cabin located between Sheldon and Field lakes, which were about one hundred miles northeast of the setttlement of Ross River. He set up a trap line and built a pit cabin on Ross River seven miles northeast of Sheldon Lake.

Sheldon Lake is unusually picturesque, with Sheldon Mountain forming a majestic backdrop for the clear waters of the lake. Northwest of the lake scattered groups of mountains form the Mackenzie Range, from which flow the Hess, the north and south forks of the Macmillan, the Rouge, the Lansing, and the Tay rivers.

North and east of Sheldon Lake the same height of land which forms the drainage for the Stewart River also provides the source for the rivers which flow eastward into the Mackenzie, such as the Twitya and the Gravel (Keele) rivers, and southward into the Liard. The prominent river flowing south is the South Nahanni, which rises in the shadows of Mount Wilson, forty miles northeast of Sheldon Lake. The peak was named for prospector Charles Wilson, whom federal geologist Joseph Keele met in the summer of 1908. Wilson had been prospecting in the area since 1905 without success, but remained in the region looking for the lost McHenry gold mine. This lost mine may also have attracted Nelson to the region. The story of the discovery first became public in 1875 when McHenry appeared at Dease Lake displaying forty pounds of gold nuggets which he said he had obtained in a placer operation somewhere northwest of Sheldon Lake. The prospector then went "outside" and never came back.*

*Joseph Keele, *Reconnaissance Across the Mackenzie Mountains*, Report No. 1097 (1910), Geological Survey of Canada, pp. 313-14. Keele refers to the lost gold mine.

Nelson hunted and trapped in this area during the winter of 1927-8. At the beginning of March 1928 Joe Ladue, Paul Sterriah, Scambella Jack, Oley Jack, Arthur John, and Jack Ladue travelled to the headwaters of the Nahanni River to hunt beaver in the vicinity of Mount Wilson. And though they passed by Nelson's cabin on the way in, they did not see him. On June 1, after a successful hunt, the Indian trappers built a moose-skin boat and floated down the Ross River. When they came to Nelson's cabin they stopped and had tea with him. Noticing that he did not have any obvious means of transportation, they asked him if he wanted to ride with them to the trading post at Ross River. He declined, though he did say a flood caused by an ice-jam had taken away his boat and much of his gear. As usual, he was uncommunicative. The men then took their leave. During much of their journey back to Ross River they discussed the man. They had noticed Nelson had no traps. Paul Sterriah was to say later that there was something odd about the man which was hard to describe. It was as if Nelson were hiding something and was afraid if visitors stayed with him for any length of time they would find out what it was.

On June 16, 1928, Nelson showed up again at Ross River. He remained there a month waiting for the supply boat *Thistle* to arrive. Nelson's actions during his stay at Ross River were no different from what they had ever been.

Another idiosyncrasy people noticed was that Nelson would never tolerate anyone walking behind him on the trail. Whenever he sensed someone following him, he would silently disappear into the forest only to reappear when the person had walked by.

When the *Thistle* finally arrived and unloaded its cargo at the Ross River post, Nelson purchased some provisions which included several boxes of .22 shells and a 30-30 Savage rifle. On July 15 he disappeared as suddenly as he had come. One day he was in his camp and the next he was gone.

People living in a small settlement such as Ross River were inclined to have strong prejudices about strangers. Nearly everyone who lived in Ross River at that time saw Nelson, and most of them considered him to be a man of hostile character, but not all. To Joe Ladue he appeared to be unsociable, but not hostile. Roy Buttle found him to be above average in his knowledge and education, and to be rational at all times. He thought Nelson to be a fairly responsive individual, and did not think of him as a sinister person. Supporting this viewpoint was the fact that he was on occasion called "Mickey": nicknames seldom accrue to totally unsociable people. This may indicate that Nelson was a man with an exaggerated range of moods, from the bellicose to the hospitable.

Arthur John, who was a youth of fourteen in 1927, remembers his uncles, Scambella Jack and Paul Sterriah, and trader Frank Etzel discussing Nelson. They believed the man was a forbidding person, and to be avoided if a man was alone when he encountered him.

The women of Ross River were generally of the same opinion. Margaret Bob recalled him as being "the silent one". To some, Nelson was the reincarnation of the "bushman"—a fearsome spectre who the Indians believe roams the bush to kill unsuspecting people. However, no one in the area disappeared, and, if indeed the trapper had victimized people, there was no evidence of it at that time.

Seven

Mayo, Lansing, and Russell Creek

AFTER LEAVING Ross River, Nelson returned to his cabin at Sheldon Lake and picked up his fur crop from the winter. He did not offer to sell any furs while at Ross post. He then journeyed north to the headwaters of the Hess River, a distance of about forty miles from his cabin. He travelled down the Hess to Twin Falls, where he suddenly met prospectors Ole Johnson, Oscar Erickson, and Norman Niddery while they were having lunch along the trail. They invited him to join them but he refused, saying he had just eaten. He told them he had built a boat at Ross River post and that he had crossed the Hess River above its confluence with the Rouge. He did not mention trapping in the Ross Lakes area, or loss of his boat. He did say his name was Arthur Nelson, and he asked how he could get to Keno, Yukon Territory. They told him, and he went on his way. Once past Twin Falls, he built a raft and floated down to Fraser Falls. Above this point on the Stewart River his life was probably saved when trader James Mervyn of Lansing Creek happened along and advised him to portage around the falls. That same day Nelson walked to Robert Levac's trading post below the cataract and asked Levac if he could stay there a few days. Levac agreed. The following day, Nelson tried to sell the trader seven marten skins, but when Levac examined the skins too closely and began to haggle over the price, Nelson impatiently swept the skins off the counter and said he would sell the skins in Mayo.

Johnson Lucas, who lived at Fraser Falls at the time, recalled that Nelson mostly stayed by himself while at the trading post, and then departed early one morning without saying a word to anyone. Lucas said that Nelson, though distant, was not unfriendly.

The silent trapper arrived in Mayo on August 25, 1928, and camped outside the town, near the Wernecke airport "hangar", as he had at Ross River. He sold his marten skins to Taylor and Drury for $680. W. H. Jeffrey, manager of the store, arranged for him to pick up his funds through the Bank of Montreal.

He remained in Mayo until September and during this time occasionally talked to Jack Alverson. Alverson was a veteran prospector and trapper who had traversed most of the drainage of the upper Stewart River on foot. As a boy, Alverson had "bar" mined on the Rogue River in Oregon. He journeyed to the Yukon in 1899, and since then had spent most of his life on the upper Stewart. In 1912, Alverson and his partner, Grant Hoffman, discovered a substantial body of silver ore after having taken a lay on the Silver King property of Galena Creek north of Mayo. Originally staked by H. W. McWhorter in 1906, the Silver King yielded $260 a ton in gold, silver, and lead. Alverson and his partner shipped fifty-nine tons in 1913 and then sold the property to Thomas P. Aitken and Henry Monroe.

Nelson learned from Alverson of the legend of another lost gold mine which supposedly existed somewhere northeast of Husky Dog River which drains into the north fork of the Macmillan near its headwaters. This story stated that two prospectors picked up gold "by the handful" on their way over to the Yukon River from Fort Norman, which is located on the Mackenzie River. They were supposed to have shown the nuggets to other prospectors they encountered on the Stewart River, but drowned in a boating accident soon afterwards. Whether the story was a "replay" of the McHenry legend or not, it attracted adventurous prospectors through the years and still does today.

Arthur Nelson was to return to Mayo several times during the next three years. The first white man to venture into the Mayo region was very similar to Nelson in his affinity for working alone. He was an indomitable New Brunswick prospector by the name of Alexander McDonald. McDonald named Mayo Lake after Alfred Mayo, one of the first traders to venture into the country after Robert Campbell. The New Brunswick man was probably the first man to ascend the Beaver River and cross into the watershed of the Wind and Peel rivers from the south. This was the same route Nelson was to follow on his trip north. McDonald was generally secretive about what he had found in the way of gold, though he would talk quite willingly about the country he had covered during his prospecting trips. Whatever knowledge of the gold wealth of the region McDonald may have had was taken with him when he died in 1894. His body was found wrapped in blankets in his camp on the banks of the Yukon River. He had apparently died in his sleep.

Numerous prospectors like McDonald spent their winters trapping to obtain a grubstake to keep them going in their never-ending search for gold. Nelson seemed to be doing the same thing, and when James Mervyn visited his camp outside Mayo in August 1928 to make a business offer, he was attentive. Mervyn offered Nelson a grubstake, two dogs, and the use of one of his trap-line cabins on the Stewart River in return for sharing the profits of any furs Nelson might trap that winter. Nelson accepted the offer and accompanied Mervyn when he went up the Stewart River. Nelson got off the boat here and Mervyn went on up the Stewart to his trading post at Lansing.

Arthur Nelson spent the winter trapping here. He was seen only once during this time and that was in March when Jack Alverson stayed overnight with him at his cabin. Nelson had little to say, though he did tell Alverson that he was of Danish extraction.

Later that month one of Mervyn's dogs strayed away from the Lansing trading post. When he reappeared a week later there was a note attached to his collar. The note was written by Nelson who explained that the dog had caught his foot in a trap. Nelson had released him after doctoring his foot with spruce gum.

The summer of 1929 saw Art Nelson camping near Lansing post for a short time. Residents of Lansing occasionally heard him singing in a ringing baritone voice as he walked down the trails in the area. This one seemingly outgoing part of his nature was not enough to cause the people who met him not to think he was an odd character. Youngsters referred to him as "The Funny Man". He rarely spoke to anyone and generally avoided contact with people living at Lansing Creek post.

Lansing Creek trading post had originally been built by Frank Braine and Percy Nash in 1902. The two men were

'98ers who returned to live at Fort Norman, N.W.T., and traded for several years with Indians who trapped in the mountains near a point where Frank Braine had camped on his way to the Klondike. They decided it would be to their advantage to move their post to the centre of the area where the "mountain" and the Mackenzie Indians trapped. Several Indian families from the Mackenzie went with them. Thus Lansing post was built near the confluence of the Stewart and Lansing rivers.

A decade later James Mervyn took over the post. In the late twenties an influenza epidemic swept the Yukon, leaving a swath of death in its wake. The Indian people were hit hard, and traders such as Mervyn were eventually forced by necessity to move.

Later in the summer of 1929, Charles Wilson—the same Wilson whom the geologist Keele had met near Sheldon Lake in 1908, and who in later years was called "Old Man Wilson"—met Nelson prospecting in the mountains east of Mayo Lake. Wilson was to recall his meeting with Nelson as a "chilling experience" which defied explanation. Wilson told the stranger about his search for the Lost McHenry mine at the headwaters of the Macmillan River. Its principal identifying characteristic was supposed to be a snow cross which formed in the summer on a mountain above a creek in which the placer gold was found. Nelson showed considerable interest, but was non-committal as to whether he too had looked for the mine or planned to look for it.

Arthur Nelson left the Stewart area toward the end of the summer of 1929. He may have heard the story of another lost mine—that of the Lost Powers gold mine—from James Mervyn before he left. This too may have been a rehashing of the same story Alverson had previously told Nelson. At any rate, when Frank Braine made the trip to the Klondike in 1898, a rumour ran rampant through the gold-rush parties who came into the Yukon via the Mackenzie River that two men, one named Powers, found gold far up the Gravel River shortly before the big gold rush.* Later, the name Powers pops up again in Dawson City, where ninety-year-old Richard Martin recounts the Powers story, but this time the gold found by Powers is located on the Miner's River branch of the Porcupine River one hundred miles northeast of the Yukon River community of Eagle, Alaska. Martin contends that Powers himself told him of finding gold under a waterfall at the headwaters of the Porcupine River. Martin recalls that Powers said he and his companion built a cabin and, weakening from scurvy, placed a sluice box containing gold on the roof before leaving. Powers was supposed to have reached Fort Yukon, Alaska, in poor condition. His partner died along the way. Powers had eighty-three pounds of alluvial gold with him and said that another eighty-five pounds lay buried in cans under a spruce tree near the cabin. He died some time afterwards. This story apparently was kindled and rekindled as the years went by and the flame has never been allowed to die. Fred Whitehead, who at seventy-nine is still searching for gold outside Chicken, Alaska, looked for this same lost mine in 1928. He and Bob Cameron followed the Tatonduk River to the north branch called Sheep Creek, and then mushed dogs up past Sheep Mountain over to the Miner's River branch of the Porcupine. Whitehead searched for the cabin and the lost mine along the Miner's River branch for a brief time, but did not find any gold. He did explore one tributary of the Miner's River called the Fishing Branch.

Still another story has the gold hidden on the headwaters of the Fifteen-Mile River only fifty miles north of Dawson City, Y.T. Yet another version of the story puts the Lost Powers Mine near the mouth of the Middle Hart

*J.G. MacGregor, *The Klondike Rush Through Edmonton*, p. 165. MacGregor discussed Braine, and Powers, and the lost gold of the Gravel River.

River. Almost certainly these stories had a direct bearing upon Nelson's later movements.

The last-named location on the Hart River was actually rediscovered in 1966 by Cyd Carr, who is currently pioneering a roadhouse at Ogilvie River on the new road being built to Fort McPherson, N.W.T., from the Yukon Territory. Carr and his associates actually found the old workings on the Hart, and though they found "good quartz", no gold was in evidence.

Whether spurred on by accounts of lost gold mines in the mountains of the height of land between the Yukon and Mackenzie drainages, or the fact that marten trapping might be better in his old haunts, Nelson journeyed back to the headwaters of the Macmillan River in 1929 to a cabin he had built in 1927 three miles south of the point where the Canol Road now crosses the Macmillan River, 130 miles northeast of Ross River. He spent the winter of 1929-30 here, and at least two people met him during this time. In February 1930 Arthur John and his trapping partner, "Captain Jinx" Johnnie, camped one night along the upper reaches of the Macmillan about three or four miles above Nelson's cabin. The two men went through the necessary steps for making a comfortable night camp. It was well past dark by the time they had a fire going and Arthur John went down to the river to chop ice for cooking supper. A full moon had come up, and in its typical eerie half-light the opposite bank of the river was illuminated. John discerned marks in the snow on the opposite bank. They were not on the trail and he wondered what creature could have made them. To his surprise, he found that they were snowshoe tracks and were quite fresh. Johnson recognized the peculiar pattern of Nelson's heavy snowshoes. He also noted that the man had apparently stood on the banks of the stream watching their camp. Whatever the reason, Nelson had turned and gone back the way he had come. Arthur John followed the tracks and found they skirted well back from the river trail. About a quarter of a mile from John's tent, Nelson's tracks showed that he had halted and waited. John surmised that Nelson figured he had alarmed the dogs of the two men and waited for them to quiet down before continuing toward their tent. Arthur John followed the tracks for about a mile and then returned to camp. He told of what he had seen to "Captain Jinx" and the two of them wondered what the lonely trapper's visit could mean, and what he was up to. The pattern of Nelson's behaviour was not customary in such a lonely stretch of country. The two men were alarmed. Johnnie pointed out that he and John had nothing of value with them, and he could see no reason for the visitor to act the way he did. John agreed but suggested that Nelson might have been listening to see what language they spoke, and on hearing that they were Indian, left them alone.

The fact that the two men were considerably worried by his actions gives substance to some of the sinister reports of Nelson's habits. Many prospectors, trappers, and miners were alike in their uneasiness in the man's presence. Arthur John and "Jinx" Johnnie remained on guard most of the night, and then broke camp early and headed south, never stopping for a day and a half. Either man could face a charging bear without quailing, but the unfathomable disposition of the silent trapper was enough to send the two men on their way with a chilling sense of foreboding.

The two men crossed to Dragon Lake and then went on to Mount Tay, where many of the Indians camped at that time of the year. They told their story, and the old and the wise of the Indian band shook their heads and wondered at the man of the silent snowshoes—was he the reincarnation of the terrifying bushman?

There was still another area which Arthur Nelson frequented during the years he wandered the headwaters of the Macmillan River. This was Russell Creek, a tributary which drains into the Macmillan a few miles down river from the confluence of the north and south forks of the river. Significantly, this was one of the few creeks in the immediate region which had produced enough gold to warrant further work.

Duncan Gillis, a Nova Scotian, had first discovered coarse gold on Russell Creek in the spring of 1898. He had come up the Gravel River and descended the Macmillan thinking that he was on the Hess (south fork of the Stewart). Gillis told Lt.-Col. Neville Armstrong of the gold prospects of what was then called Slate Creek. Armstrong bought out Gillis's interest in Russell Creek. He prospected the stream for two decades and finally promoted a hydraulic operation there in 1926, but gold was not found in large enough quantities to continue operating, and Armstrong left the creek never to return.*

Thanks to Armstrong's influence (he was the son of an English baronet), Russell Creek became well known during the first two decades of the twentieth century for its big-game hunting. For example, in 1904, world-renowned hunters F. C. Selous and Charles Sheldon used Armstrong's camp as a base for hunting in the area. Accompanying the hunters were W. H. Osgood of the U.S. Biological Survey, who named the Nelson sheep after another member of the Survey, and famous artist Carl Rungius. Four of these men wrote books which included passages about the region; thus by the time Arthur Nelson arrived in the area Russell Creek had had considerable publicity even though it was sparsely settled.

Arthur Zimmerlie had built a trading post at the mouth of Russell Creek in the early twenties to accommodate trappers who moved into the upper Macmillan to take advantage of rising fur prices. This included supplying Indians who lived at Husky Dog Town located near the

*Armstrong was not always at the creek. During the First World War he trained snipers and scouts for the Canadian Expeditionary Force.

mouth of the Husky Dog River where it drains into the north fork of the Macmillan.

Besides the influx of trappers, a small gold stampede resulted in 1927 following Armstrong's promotion of his placer operation. If Arthur Nelson journeyed specifically to Russell Creek seeking gold, he remained on the fringes of the rush, and no one was able to pinpoint the day or month of his arrival. Joe Menzies encountered Nelson in the summer of 1929 in the low pass which runs from Twin Falls on the Hess to the Macmillan River. Menzies put it aptly when he once said of Nelson, "If a man never says anything, how are you going to know where he's been, where he lives, or where he's going!"

Yet another lost gold-mine story cropped up at this time in this region. Gerry Kelley and his wife Rose had a trapping cabin twenty-five miles up the south fork of the Macmillan from the Russell Creek post, or about seventy-five miles down river from Nelson's cabin. Rose is the daughter of J. F. Hosfall, and granddaughter of Leroy "Jack" McQuesten, a pioneer trader who came into the Yukon in 1873. McQuesten and his partners, Arthur Harper and Alfred Mayo, were to become famous in the north country for grubstaking prospectors through the years, and through their efforts were indirectly responsible for the discovery of gold by George Carmack on Bonanza Creek in 1896, and the subsequent Klondike gold rush.

The Kelleys had heard of a lost gold mine to the northeast, and in the summer of 1928 backpacked across a trail which left the south Macmillan immediately across from their cabin and ran forty miles north to Husky Dog Town. From here, they were going to travel up the Husky Dog River to search for a fabulous placer ground which an Indian by the name of "Souca" had told them about. Souca, who is now in his nineties, vaguely recalled this ground to be between the upper reaches of the Husky Dog

River and the Mackenzie mountains. However, a lack of supplies forced the Kelleys to turn back. Later that summer they moved out of their cabin on the south fork of the Macmillan. Kelley took over as a relief operator on the telegraph line at Stewart City, a small settlement located at the confluence of the Stewart and Yukon rivers. Though Nelson had been through the Russell Creek and Hess River regions, Rose Kelley did not recall seeing him up to the time she and her husband moved in August 1928. However, Mrs. Ben Joe, who at that time lived at Husky Dog Town, recalls being with a group of people who suddenly met Nelson on a path near Husky Dog Town. Nelson jumped off the trail and darted into the bush like a startled animal. His actions scared her. Such incidents were to happen several more times to other residents of that area over the next two years.

At some time in the period when Arthur Nelson roamed the Russell Creek region, he is believed to have built a cabin on a small lake at the headwaters of Russell Creek. The structure was more of a dugout than a cabin, with a pit being dug and rimmed with logs and a split-log roof covered with sod capping the structure. Snoose Benson, who now lives on the Ogilvie River where it is crossed by the Dempster Road, lived in the cabin after Nelson. John Haydon, of Whitehorse, also stayed in the cabin in 1938 while journeying from his trap line on the Husky Dog River to Dawson City. In 1962, the pit cabin was still in evidence when prospectors Jack Simpson and Jack Smith of Whitehorse, and John O'Neil of Ross River, searched the Russell Creek area for signs of mineralization.

Several times during the period Nelson lived in the upper Macmillan and Russell Creek regions, he purchased supplies from Arthur Zimmerlie at his trading post. On one occasion he bought shotgun shells. On another occasion, Sam Isaac, a local Indian trapper, happened to be in the store when Nelson walked in, and he at first thought the man was unable to talk, since the stranger pointed at various items he wanted and said not a word. Isaac was to meet the man again on the upper reaches of Russell Creek where, characteristically, Nelson walked by him without saying a word.

In the spring of 1930, Nelson appeared at Russell Creek trading post before break-up and purchased some supplies. He bought a canoe from Pete Frederickson, a Swedish trapper and prospector who lived at Russell Creek with his partner, Pete Linder, another Swede. As usual, Nelson camped a good distance away from the settlement. Linder, however, went up to say hello to the visitor. Nelson was sitting in front of a small cooking fire when Linder walked up. Nelson appeared to be in a friendly mood and waved to Linder to sit down. At this point Linder noticed that the trapper had a new rifle leaning against a tree, and walked over and hefted it in his hands. "Nice rifle you got here. Brand new," Pete said without bothering to look around. Then it dawned on Linder that there was an ominous silence behind him. He turned slightly and glanced out of the corner of his eye just in time to see Nelson slowly pull his hand up from his side and put it across his chest under his coat. There was no hiding the movement and Linder judged that it was done with the intention that he, Linder, should see it. Linder realized immediately that if he made one precipitous move with the rifle, Nelson would probably be ready with a pistol or sawed-off gun of some kind. Pete carefully put the gun down, and Nelson dropped his hand and motioned for Linder to sit down. "Have some tea," Nelson offered.

Linder sat down, and a few minutes later was joined by Pete Frederickson and Anton Leland, another trapper and prospector who frequented that region. Linder, Frederickson, and Leland did most of the talking while Nelson seemed content to sit back and listen. Finally, he stood up and began sorting and packing supplies he had purchased from Zimmerlie at the Russell Creek post. When this was completed he silently gave each man an orange—a valuable item in the back country in those days—and then stepped into the boat he had recently purchased from Frederickson. "See you," he said and shoved off, poling out the nearby slough.

"Thanks for the orange," Linder yelled after him, but Nelson kept to his task, not bothering to acknowledge Linder's remark.

Frederickson looked at his orange, and then looked at Leland and Linder and said, "Kind of a funny guy, eh!" The other two nodded in agreement while they stared after the stranger as he poled up river.

Eight

The Lost Porcupine Mine

ARTHUR NELSON'S next appearance was at Ross River in July of 1930. He met the Taylor and Drury supply boat *Yukon Rose* on July 13, 1930, and in so doing was photographed by the pilot of the craft, Frank Slim. Slim had been coming into Ross River for five years, first on the *Thistle*, and then, after it sank in 1928, on the *Rose*. Each year, Frank, out of habit, would take a photo of the Taylor and Drury supply house from the deck of the boat. Thus, this particular year he photographed Nelson standing next to Anglican missionary preacher John Martin. Martin, who was from the northern Yukon, had been ordained two years earlier in Aklavik, N.W.T., and from there had journeyed to Dawson City, and then in March of 1930 had gone by dog sled to Ross River. During the trip Martin's wife helped deliver a baby born to the Van Bibber family at their home on the Pelly River.

The fact that Nelson was standing next to Martin in the photo may indicate that Martin told him the story of the Lost Powers mine on the Miner's River in northern Yukon. Martin was the first man to guide the famous Royal North West Mounted Police patrols between Dawson City and Fort McPherson. He knew the upper Peel country well and like his older brother Richard knew the Powers story. Martin may also have suggested the area of the Peel River as a good place to try trapping. Whatever was said, Nelson got on the supply boat and rode it as far as Fort Selkirk. Frank Slim, who recalled meeting Nelson on the Lapie River in 1927 and again at Ross River in the summer of 1928, said Nelson told him he was going down river to Dawson City. After arriving at Dawson, Nelson is believed to have worked for a month patrolling the twelve-mile ditch. This was built to supply water for the Yukon Consolidated Gold Company operation seven miles outside of Dawson City. One Indian from Old Crow, Yukon Territory, who worked on the twelve-mile ditch that summer said the new man used the name Al Johnson and said he was going to trap that winter on the headwaters of the Peel River.

Nelson next appeared twenty miles down river from Dawson at a place called Half Way. Percy DeWolfe, known as "The Iron Man of the Yukon" for his years of driving a mail sled between Dawson City and Eagle, had a fishing camp at Half Way which he ran with his two sons, Walter and William. Some time in August, Nelson stopped at the fishing camp and ate lunch with the DeWolfes. He was non-committal as to where he was going. DeWolfe gave him a salmon to help with his larder. As well as his being a quiet man, William and Walter recall that Nelson had a Scandinavian accent.

The trapper went on down river to Eagle. Here he met Dolphus Charley and Forty Mile Billy at Charley Creek. They told him that he had gone past his destination when he asked how far it was to the Tatonduk River. Nelson then poled back up the Yukon River and lined his boat up the Tatonduk and Sheep Creek, the same route Fred Whitehead had taken in 1928. Joe Malcolm, who owned a trap line up the Tatonduk and Eagle Creek, recalled the stranger working his way upstream. Later, to Malcolm's amazement, he found the boat at the forks of Sheep Creek, above the canyon of the creek. To this day neither Indians nor whites who have seen this boat above the canyon can figure how he got it up there, and there the boat still lies. The canyon, or really, series of canyons, is characterized by projecting overhangs so steep that in places men mushing their dogs in winter cannot see the sky. In addition, the mountains on both sides of the canyon are so precipitous that it would be absolutely impractical and nearly impossible for one man to drag a wooden boat up in the way Nelson appears to have done. Giving credibility to the story is the fact that Whitehead did not see the boat when he went up the creek by dog team in the spring of 1928, though of course it may have been covered with snow. Local Indians point out that they would have built a skin boat rather than bother carrying a wooden boat above the canyon.

Arthur Nelson was never seen again in Eagle. His route indicated that he may have been heading for the Lost Porcupine Mine on the Miner's River, and after exploring that area of the upper Porcupine he may have drifted across the headwaters of the Ogilvie to the Hart River, following that up until he gained the headwaters of the Klondike River.

From this point a trail led down to the Mayo Road and familiar territory. He spent the winter of 1930-1 back at the headwaters of the Macmillan River. Arthur Zimmerlie claimed to have counted Nelson in March 1931 while taking the census at Russell Creek.

In mid-April 1931 Arthur Nelson suddenly showed up on the Mayo-Keno Road and was given a ride to Mayo by Bud Fisher. In keeping with his regular habit, the stranger camped in a tent near the Wernecke Airport hangar, and on three occasions purchased supplies from Archie Currie, former member of the R.C.M.P., who was then working in Binet's store. Currie noticed that the man was generally uncommunicative, but he was a good customer. He knew what he wanted and ordered it with little fanfare. He had plenty of cash to pay for his purchases.

Currie did not forget the man because he ordered an entire year's supply of Beecham's pills. There were fifty pills in a box and twelve boxes in a package. Two boxes had already been sold when Nelson bought the remaining boxes of the package. Nelson was deadly serious when he purchased the huge supply and Currie did not pry into a customer's reasons for obtaining articles. The unusual order, however, did have the effect of registering the man in Currie's mind, and he did not forget him. Currie judged Nelson to be thirty-six or thirty-seven years old, possibly more. "I remember his face being lined," Currie was to recall, "and that he wasn't a very tall man—I would say he was around five feet seven or eight."

The presence of the silent stranger was not long in being known. Even in those days it was not a common thing to see a man camp on the outskirts of the small river town, especially when a hotel was available at reasonable rates. Youngsters pointed to the man, and adults engaged in conversations about him in an attempt to find out what made the man so unsociable.

He remained at Mayo for four or five days and then

walked north along the road to Keno. He carried a huge pack on his back which John Kinman was to describe later. Karl Kimbel was driving an ore truck to Keno when he came upon Nelson walking along the side of the road. Kimbel stopped the truck and asked the man if he wanted a ride. The trapper refused, shaking his head. He did not utter a sound. Kimbel shrugged and drove off.

Nelson walked to the foot of Keno Hill where he stayed a few nights in a cabin located just off the Mayo-Keno road. The cabin still stands today, though the roof has caved in. While living here, Nelson occasionally walked up the hill to purchase supplies from Dick O'Loane of Northern Commercial Company, and from Joe Clifton at the Taylor and Drury store.

On May 3 he asked John "Hard Rock" MacDonald and John Vine Sullivan how he could get to Fort McPherson in the Northwest Territories. "Hard Rock" had already walked to Fort McPherson, a distance of 350 miles, several times. He pointed north and told Nelson to take the trail to Silver Hill. Sullivan told the trapper that he was going north along the trail with his partner, Walter Johnson, and said Nelson could accompany them if he chose. Nelson agreed. The next day the three men got a late start and camped near Crystal Creek. That night the men built a fire, but Nelson refused to sit with Johnson and Sullivan, choosing rather to remain by himself thirty yards down the trail. During the time he was with Sullivan and Johnson, Nelson sat alone, staring straight ahead of him. He said not a word and hefted his 30-30 Savage in his hands in an ominous manner. Sullivan and Johnson rolled out their sleeping bags and strove to get some sleep, but the thought of the strange man sitting but a short way down the trail silently hefting a rifle was not conducive to much rest. The next morning when they awoke, he was gone.

A short time after leaving Johnson and Sullivan, Nelson met Frank Gillespie while he was preparing breakfast, but the trapper declined to share Gillespie's meal, saying that he was going on to Haggart Creek. He did not go that way. Here Nelson may have erred. By missing this trail, he missed the route to the Hart River. The Porcupine River could eventually be gained by a two-day portage from the point where the Hart flows into the upper Peel. Possibly in error, he continued along the trail to where he met John Kinman, and ultimately ended up on the Wind River.

Part Three

Tracing the Trapper

Nine

Nelson alias Johnson?

BLOW-UPS OF THE photo taken by Frank Slim of Arthur Nelson at Ross River were sent to Fort McPherson, where Andrew Kunnezi and John Robert confirmed Nelson's likeness to Albert Johnson. However, not all are in complete agreement on this. Abe Francis, who sold Johnson a canoe, believes that Johnson was taller than the man shown in the photo standing next to John Martin.

Unfortunately, the photo was taken at some distance

and, though clear, loses much facial detail when it is blown up to a point where a man could give a definite confirmation that Nelson and Johnson were the same person.

Thus, in order to cast the balance one way or the other numerous questions must be asked and answered. Were the men similar psychologically? Were any possessions found on Johnson when he was killed traceable to Nelson? Were the men similar in habits and abilities? Each subject must be taken on its own weight and analysed.

Possessions

Of all the items found in Albert Johnson's possession when he was killed, the most logical ones to trace were his weapons. The author wrote to Superintendent R. P. Stone, commander of the Depot Division of the Royal Canadian Mounted Police at Regina, Saskatchewan, for the serial numbers of Johnson's Iver Johnson shotgun, his 30-30 Savage rifle, and his Winchester .22.

In answer to this letter, written September 14, 1969, the commander of the Depot Division reported that the Winchester .22 did not have a serial number. The curator of the R.C.M.P. museum, Malcolm Wake, confirmed this with Staff Sgt. S. J. Kirby, one of the Force's firearms experts, who said this is in keeping with general policies of firearms manufacturers in regards to inexpensive weapons. (The firing mechanism of the .22 was jammed with the bolt action open. It is not known if the gun was jammed at the time Johnson was killed.)

The information about the rifle was relayed to the Winchester Arms Company in a letter sent October 19, 1969. Winchester replied that there were no records kept on inexpensive, lower-power weapons.

The Iver Johnson Champion 16-gauge shotgun which

Johnson purchased in Fort McPherson would be of no assistance in identifying Nelson and Johnson as one and the same.

The Royal Canadian Mounted Police supplied the serial number of the 30-30 Savage which was found in Johnson's hands when he was killed. The serial number, 292575, was forwarded by the author to Robert McComb, Works Manager of the Savage Arms Company plant in Westfield, Massachusetts. On November 4, 1969, Mr. McComb wrote back that he had checked the records of the Savage and found that the rifle was a Model 99-30-30F, the "F" indicating it to be a "featherweight" model. He sent a photocopy of the shipping manifest showing that the rifle was sent to Marshall Wells Company on May 2, 1927. Mr. McComb added that he believed it was sent to Marshall Wells Limited in Canada and said his company still does business with the Canadian firm.

Const. Claude Tidd, who served with the R.C.M.P. in Ross River and Mayo, investigated the Johnson case in 1933. His report stated that Roy Buttle, manager of the Taylor and Drury store in Ross River, sold a 30-30 Savage rifle to Arthur Nelson on or about June 30, 1928. Significantly, the largest customer of Marshall Wells Company in northern Canada at that time was Taylor and Drury. Their records, as well as the records of Marshall Wells, have been destroyed, but the indications are strong that T & D was the recipient of the rifle which was sold to Nelson, and which was later found in Johnson's hands. As far as can be determined by the author, the rifle never before had been traced from the Savage Arms Company to Marshall Wells Company.

Also of considerable importance in relation to the rifle in linking the identity of Johnson and Nelson was John Kinman's observation that Nelson was carrying a Savage 250-3000 before he crossed Braine Pass. This model is easily identified. The fact that Kinman mistook the calibre does not detract from his statement; without calipers it would be difficult to tell the difference in the calibre. The fact that the two men were carrying like weapons adds to the overall picture of them being one man.

Another item of importance was the pills found on Johnson. Nelson had purchased five hundred pills the preceding spring. Trappers do carry pills, but the fact that Johnson had in his possession thirty-seven pills of the same type also adds to the probability of identification.

Sgt. James R. Purdie of the R.C.M.P.'s Dawson detachment traced the currency found in Johnson's possession. One $50 bill was traced to a shipment of bills received by the Bank of Montreal in Dawson City on September 7, 1926, and another $50 bill was traced to the Mayo branch as part of a shipment of one hundred such bills on March 22, 1928.

Other possessions found on Albert Johnson which were in keeping with the scanty history of Nelson were the five pearls, loose gold, and unusually large snowshoes.

Arthur Nelson on several occasions had mentioned to Edward Asp that he had once been a seaman, which could account for the pearls. In respect to the gold, Nelson frequented areas of placer mining operations and could be expected to have loose gold on his person. As for the snowshoes, Arthur John identified Nelson on the Macmillan by the size and weight of his snowshoes and the peculiar double webbing under the heel, which were in keeping with the cumbersome pair worn by Johnson.

Still another similarity were the pit cabins built by Nelson and the one in which Johnson lived.

Albert Johnson was in possession of a compass. This was a common article for men who walked long distances in the bush; therefore this item would not have been signicant in identifying him as Arthur Nelson. The compass in Johnson's possession was believed to have been purchased at Fort McPherson.

An oddity was a similarity in what Johnson and Nelson did not have. Those who tracked down Johnson during the shoot-out uncovered the fact that he had neither dogs nor traps. The same applied to Nelson when he was visited by the Indians returning from the South Nahanni in the spring of 1928. Nelson said that his gear was lost in a flood. Of course, many trappers resorted to deadfalls and snares, and carried their supplies without the use of dogs. The very weight of steel traps would be a hindrance for a man without dogs. This similarity of habit in regard to the possessions of the two men, though not conclusive, assists in establishing that they were the same.

Physical Likeness

Four death photographs were taken of Albert Johnson. The principal objections to the identification value of these are that he had undergone considerable privation before his death. Loss of weight and frozen facial extremities resulted in a partially distorted picture of what he really looked like. Continued exposure to the extreme cold seems to have distorted his nose and ears. His mouth is open in what Wop May considered to be a sneer, but more likely it is a grimace as the result of being hit by rifle bullets.

Two profile shots point up one physical characteristic of Johnson which stands out more than any other: Johnson had either one ear frozen or two unlike ears—a not uncommon physical trait. Johnson's hair also shows a cowlick.

The author was able to interview eight people who had seen Arthur Nelson, and to present them with the death photos for identification.* Tom Coleman had only seen

*Besides those mentioned here, Johnson Lucas, Fred Berg, and Sam Isaac recognized the man they knew as Arthur Nelson.

Nelson once and that was very briefly in the Northern Commercial Company store in Keno. He thought that Johnson could be the same man as Nelson, but disclaimed his irrefutability as a reference.

Archie Currie, who sold Nelson the five hundred pills, said there were some similarities, and though the face seemed to be distorted, he believed it to be Nelson.

One of the more unassailable identifications was obtained when the author sent an unlabelled picture each to Arthur John and Joe Ladue in Ross River, Y.T. A month after sending the pictures, the two men were asked if they could identify the man. Both Ladue and John were interrogated at different times and places, and both were unhesitating in stating bluntly that Johnson and Nelson were one and the same person. They both gave the same reason for being able to identify the man. They said they would never forget the man's eyes. Ladue and John probably saw more of Nelson (with the exception of James Mervyn) than anyone after he left Dease Lake.

Mrs. Laura Moi, daughter of John Vile Sullivan, remembers seeing Nelson with her father. She recalled that Arthur Nelson was an extremely shy man. In 1933 she was shown the death photo by Claude Tidd of the Mounties. There was no doubt in her mind that Albert Johnson and Arthur Nelson were the same. She also contends that the Frank Slim photo proves Nelson and Johnson were the same man.

As has been previously mentioned, Buck and George Adsit and Ed Asp identified Johnson as being Nelson when they saw his picture in the *True Detective Mysteries Magazine* issues of October and November of 1932.

Another interesting identification was made by Gus Kraus, who has been a game warden and trapper in the vicinity of Nahanni Butte, N.W.T., and the drainage of the South Nahanni River for fifty years. He was sent an unlabelled picture, and he wrote back that the man in the photograph had a striking resemblance to a cranky Finn by the name of Gus Leafie, who trapped at Bistcho Lake in northwestern Alberta immediately south of Nahanni Butte in 1925. Kraus went on to say that Leafie told him he had once been a seaman and had fished for wages out of Vancouver. He left Bistcho Lake area suddenly in 1925, saying that he was going to try fishing in Alaska. Kraus said that Leafie had a tattoo on one arm, which would seem to rule out the theory that Leafie and Johnson were the same man. The physician's report stated that Johnson had no "operation" scars or natural marks on his body. It would seem that "scars" would include tattoos, and it is highly doubtful that a tattoo would be overlooked unless a bullet shattered the spot where the tattoo was present. One odd factor here is the failure of Dr. Urquhart to report a vaccination scar and also an apparent pockmark on Johnson's right cheek. It would appear very unlikely that a man between thirty-five and forty years old could get through life without having a vaccination.

Former Game Warden Phillip Brown, who with Skook Davidson was mentioned in Richmond Hobson's best-selling books about the Chilcotin country of northern British Columbia, reported that there was a resemblance between the man of the photo and a rancher and trapper by the name of Anton Nelson who lived on Greer Creek southwest of Vanderhoof, B.C., from 1913 to his death in 1945. He said that Anton Nelson kept three or four cocked and loaded rifles in his cabin at all times, and that on many occasions he threatened the lives of his neighbours who complained to Brown and the police about the man. Brown figured that Anton Nelson was mentally unbalanced, and in his letter he said, "The picture looks like Anton Nelson, but the man is not old enough, and besides, the Nelson I knew was never known to smile." Further investigation turned up the fact that Anton Nelson was seventy-six when he died in 1945, which would have meant that he was sixty-three in 1932, or twenty-three years older than the maximum age suggested by Dr. Urquhart in his estimate of Albert Johnson. Whether Anton Nelson may have been related to Arthur Nelson has not been determined. Extensive investigation on the part of the author has turned up no facts on Anton Nelson other than that he came from the United States in 1906, and that he had been an immigrant from Norway.

Thus, the photos, though helpful, were by themselves inconclusive in establishing the fact that Johnson was Nelson. Other than the actual photographs of Johnson there is little to go by in comparing the two physically except for their height, and on this point there is a marked difference between the two. Measurement as put forth by Dr. Urquhart has Johnson being 5'9½" tall. To a man, every person in the Yukon Territory and British Columbia who was interviewed said he believed Nelson was not that tall. This difference may be attributed to the fact that Johnson was measured after he was dead. Since Nelson has generally been accredited with walking with stooped shoulders, this may explain why those who knew him thought that he was shorter than he actually was.

As to age, both men were estimated to be between thirty-five and forty years old.

If Nelson had an accent, it was very slight, indicating that he was almost certainly second generation or had been brought to North America when he was an infant. Roy Buttle recognized the faintest trace of a Scandinavian accent. Archie Currie noticed no accent. As far as can be determined concerning Albert Johnson, no accent was detected. The Asp family of Dease Lake said that Nelson spoke Swedish, and, as Edward Asp was from Sweden, this would indicate that Arthur Nelson's parents were from Sweden. Somewhat conflicting is Jack Alverson's statement that Nelson said he was Danish. Of course, there is a possibility that one of Nelson's parents or grandparents had been from Denmark. No information is available with regard to Johnson's origin from the Fort McPherson area.

The behaviour of Johnson and of Nelson is one of the more important facets in proving that the two men were one and the same. With the exception of Nelson's penchant for an occasional game of poker while working at Dease Lake, the two men are almost perfectly interchangeable. (Even in playing poker, Nelson was withdrawn.) Johnson, in the short time he was known at Fort McPherson, startled local residents with his unsocial manner. He was evasive with police, camped outside of the settlement, avoided people, was forthright in his purchase of supplies, and departed without announcement.

Similarly, Nelson was remembered to be of an unsocial nature. He evaded police in Mayo and Keno, and camped outside of the towns of Mayo and Ross River. He was judged to be a "no fooling" type of customer by merchants who dealt with him at Mayo, Keno, Ross River, and Russell Creek. He generally avoided people wherever he went, and seldom talked with anyone.

Albert Johnson was judged to be a good man with an axe, as was Arthur Nelson, especially by those who saw him working at Dease Lake. Johnson was a crack shot. Nelson, in turn, could work a lever action with lightning speed, as he showed while with Asp.

Johnson proved his physical ability while eluding the police for thirty-eight days on the trail. Nelson's speed in avoiding Coleman in wet snow on the Wind River trail indicated that he would have been capable of Johnson's feats of endurance.

The available data constitute a fairly good case for Albert Johnson's being Arthur Nelson. The other routes to the Peel River were checked to see if a man similar to Johnson passed by prior to June 1931, and not one has presented a lead. These include Fort Yukon at the mouth of the Porcupine and located in Alaska, Fort Good Hope and Fort Norman on the Mackenzie River in the Northwest

Territories, and Aklavik and Herschel Island on the Arctic Ocean.

All leads point to Mayo and Keno in the Yukon Territory, and to Arthur Nelson. Unfortunately, the information on Nelson was not forthcoming until over a year after Johnson was killed. In view of the condition of communications at that time, it is not surprising that Nelson appeared in the picture so late. For example, Const. Claude Tidd mushed into Whitehorse, Y.T., in the spring of 1929 from his post at Ross River, and the trip was duly reported in the local newspaper, the *Whitehorse Star*. The article included a statement by Tidd in which he pointed out that he had not received any type of communication from Whitehorse since the previous June, almost a year earlier.

Mail from Mayo and Ross River took over two months between the time it was dispatched and the time an answer was received. Anyone investigating the case would have needed the patience of Job and life expectancy of Methuselah to complete it successfully.

Besides the trouble afforded investigators by the poor communications of the day was the fact that Nelson was called Johnson when he appeared at Fort McPherson. This effectively disguised Nelson's identity, and any relatives or friends who would have pictured Nelson as being Johnson during the fifty-four-day "Arctic War" were thrown off the track by the name change. There is little likelihood that these same people eventually would have heard about the Mounties' tracing Johnson to Nelson in the Yukon Territory because by then eighteen months had gone by and it was almost an aside to the vast publicity which had gone before.

Still another factor which contributed to the complexity of the entire case was the fact that Nelson was only traced as far as Ross River. That Nelson had spent some time at Dease Lake, B.C., had never officially come to light until the author uncovered it in 1968, though, of course, Dease

Lake residents had known about it for years. This was a most important factor because it proved the *veracity* of Nelson's statements to trader Roy Buttle in Ross River in late summer of 1927. If Nelson apparently told the truth about his itinerary, he more than likely was telling the truth about his name. This, in turn, could eventually be of value in proving his origin and identity.

Ten

The Search for a Past

BASED ON evidence submitted that Albert Johnson and Arthur Nelson were the same individual, who then was this man? In forty years not even the Royal Canadian Mounted Police, which is generally accredited as the finest all-round police force in the world, has come up with the answer.

The author has to admit failure after attempting to identify Johnson. Even with improved communications such as television and jet mail service, the mystery of Albert Johnson's identity is still as baffling today as it was four decades ago.

After a review of basic clues, the rest must be left up to the reader.

The first thing looked for when a person dies in a remote place is his identification. In most cases the average individual has a wallet containing identity cards. If these are not present other items are sought such as a locket, or letters, anything on which there may be an address, name, or serial number which provide the opportunity for tracing the person.

In the case of Albert Johnson, there was not one item which could be traced farther than Fort McPherson, N.W.T., other than his 30-30 Savage rifle. And the Savage was only of use in proving that Nelson probably was Johnson. Nelson purchased the Savage in Ross River, but this knowledge is of no help in proving where he came from previously.

Five pearls were found in Johnson's possession. It is not known if they were salt-water or fresh-water pearls.* They do point to the possibility of Albert Johnson's having once frequented a sea coast or an inland lake.

Placer gold found in Johnson's possession indicates that he prospected and panned for gold. In some areas, prospectors and placer miners can judge which creek placer gold came from by its shape, but Johnson had covered such a huge area in his wanderings that this was deemed impossible.

Albert Johnson's snowshoes were homemade, and ruggedly built, but their design is so general as to be of little use in determining where Johnson was from. Common to the Loucheux is a shoe with a round front end. However, they also make pointed snowshoes similar to John-

*Fresh-water pearls are found in Great Slave Lake and Lake Athabaska, both bodies of water being loosely associated with Johnson's past.

son's, though much lighter and more refined. One prevalent rumour in the Northern Yukon was that the webbing on Johnson's snowshoes was made out of wire, but the photo of the shoes dispels that theory.

The trapper had thirty-two pills in three small packages. These point to Arthur Nelson's purchase of Beecham's pills in Mayo, but are of no help in tracing the man's "outside" identity.

The only other known item which would be of some value if it could be traced was the .38 calibre revolver left at Thibert Creek by Arthur Nelson. The Asp family had this in their possession for many years, but when they moved from their Porter's Landing home to a new location across Dease Lake, the weapon was either lost, or stolen by drifters boating through the area.

The remainder of Johnson's possessions are of no help in determining his past. His clothes, for example, were either made from skins, purchased in Fort McPherson, or had no labels.

With Johnson's possessions bereft of clues, the only other course to follow is to review his personal habits, characteristics, and physical appearance and ability for suggestions of his past.

Of no small importance is the fact that when members of the posse searched the trapper's cabin and surrounding area after the January 9 shoot-out, they found that Johnson had dug a slit trench for a latrine. Army veterans of the posse surmised from this that Albert Johnson was a veteran of some army, somewhere. Also, his lack of panic when dynamite was thrown at his cabin indicated possible experience under shell fire.

Since two estimates of the trapper's age were thirty-five and forty when he was killed in 1932, this would have put his birth date between 1892 and 1897, a perfect military age for service in the First World War.

Still another clue pointing to war service was a possible

scar showing on the fugitive's right cheek in his death photos. Retired Detective Sgt. Ralph Godfrey, of the Oakland, California, police force, perused the death photo and a dental chart based on official R.C.M.P. records, and suggested that this mark might have resulted from an old bullet wound. He supported this hypothesis by noting the four teeth missing from Johnson's right upper jaw. Godfrey also noted that his jaw seemed to bulge as though permanently dislocated and pushed out by the impact of a missile of some kind, and that the disfiguration caused by the wound quite possibly could be the psychological impetus which drove Johnson into isolation. Of course, the scar (if it was a scar) might not have been the result of a bullet wound. It could have come from a bout with a skin disease. Also, quite possibly it might have been a blemish incurred during the transporting of Johnson's body after he was killed, and be of no value in identification.

Earl Hersey said the men of the posse who were experienced trappers commented that they did not think Johnson was knowledgeable as a trapper. Curiously, no traps were found in or near Johnson's cabin. However, his traps may have been dispersed through the bush, and he also may have used deadfalls and snares.

Albert Johnson was a crack shot with a rifle, one point all the men agreed on, and they judged that he was also expert with a handgun because of the way he handled the sawed-off shotgun and .22 rifle during the January 9 shootout. He also appeared to be skilled with an axe.

When the pursuit of Johnson continued week after week, the men of the posse began to realize that the fugitive's greatest asset was his incredible stamina and physical capability.

Additional clues supplied by Nelson's conversations with various people of British Columbia and the Yukon were that he had been a logger and a miner at one time in his life. His almost superhuman physical ability could only have come as the result of the life of continuous toil demanded by such occupations. In addition, he may have worked on a farm in North Dakota as a youth.

Nelson was a good singer, and could play the harmonica. He was never observed to take a drink, nor did he smoke. He was known to have taken snuff.

Recollections as to whether "The Mad Trapper of Rat River" had a Scandinavian accent are so diverse as to be inconclusive in determining his origin.

The foregoing clues may be considered in light of the following "leads" the author has obtained.

Pilot Wop May wrote an article in *True Detective Mysteries Magazine* in 1932 wherein he said he thought Albert Johnson was a man named "Coyote Bill" who was wanted in the state of Idaho for the murder of the superintendent of an irrigation company in 1930. The principal reason for May's opinion was that a photo of the man showed a strong likeness to Johnson. Nothing ever came of this lead.

Hank Lee, Sam and Jim Deckert, and Milford Patchal trapped with a man by the name of Arthur Nelson in the spring of 1926 near Ebenezer, Saskatchewan. Lee, who now resides in Dawson City, described this man as being a crack shot with a .22 pistol and also as carrying a .38 calibre Smith and Wesson revolver. He said that Nelson was a quiet person. However, he did recall Nelson once mentioning that he had been in the Black Hills country of the Dakotas. In a letter to the author, Mrs. Joe Deckert, who lives in Yorkton, Saskatchewan, said that "Albert Johnson" "batched" with her brother-in-law Jim Deckert on the Sam Deckert ranch. She said that "Johnson" was a man of good character. She did not say where he came from. Hank Lee recalled that "Johnson" was called Art Nelson when he knew him. Lee described Nelson as being about 5'11" tall and having light brown hair. He said Nelson had a habit of brushing his hair back by simultaneously running both hands along the sides of his head. The significance of this is that Lee noted the tufts of Nelson's hair sticking out on both sides of the back of his head when shown the Ross River photo. Lee recalled Nelson to be about twenty-three years old in 1926, which would put him at only twenty-nine when he was killed, or considerably younger than the Mounties' estimate of Albert Johnson's age.

James Deckert was contacted at his home in Detroit, Michigan. Death photos of Johnson were sent to him. He said he believes Albert Johnson's real name was Edward Buckman. Deckert hunted muskrat with Buckman on the White Sand River north of Yorkton, Saskatchewan, in the fall of 1925. He said Buckman on one occasion went out of his way to avoid a Mountie who was on patrol. Buckman told Deckert he had once lived in British Columbia.

A man who lives in the Yukon but prefers to remain anonymous said that he met a man named Albert Johnson in Prince Rupert, B.C., about 1926. He said this man matches the photos he saw after Albert Johnson was killed. He recalled Johnson's saying that he had once been a seaman and that he jumped ship in New York when he came to North America. He remembers Johnson's mentioning Portland, Oregon, and also that he had worked for a short time with the Cable Car Company in San Francisco. The Yukoner recalls that Johnson said he was Norwegian.

Nelson's statement that he was raised on a farm fits the following lead: he was thought to have worked on the Rezenchenko Ranch near Maple Creek, Saskatchewan, in the twenties. Another interesting piece of information about this area—though it has nothing to do with the Rezenchenko Ranch—is that some of the first big-scale rustling of cattle by truck was done in this area in the twenties.

Earl Hersey, last man shot by Johnson, is of the opinion that Johnson was "a gunman from Chicago"! Johnson died the typical death of the "Chicago-style" gunman. That is: he never was to say a word, he was loaded down with ammunition and guns, he had no identification on him, and he fought to the death.

A lead in the Dawson City area has Johnson a man named Joe Miller, who supposedly murdered a woman while taking her down the Yukon River in a boat to the Kuskokwin River in Alaska.

One of the oddest leads of all has Art Nelson connected with a man named Peterson who was found dead under suspicious circumstances in the spring of 1925 in his cabin at Black Lake in northern Saskatchewan. A Yukon trapper, Harvey MacKibbon, told the author that he knew two brothers, Ben and Einar Paulsen, one of whom trapped near Black Lake. He said that one of the brothers knew a man there named Arthur Nelson. The Yukon man did not know the other part of this lead which the author had heard, and that was that a man by the name of Arthur Nelson left the Black Lake area suddenly about 1925 and was never seen again. By the time Peterson's body was found it was nothing more than a skeleton. An empty liquor bottle was found on his chest. Local trappers were convinced there had been foul play in the Peterson case, and this seemed to be substantiated when trapper Oscar Johnson found Peterson's trunk in the bushes on the shore of Middle Lake (some distance away from Black Lake) nine years later!* An interesting tie-in with this possibility came from ex-Mountie Tom Sturgeon who said that he heard Nelson's bitterness was caused by the fact that his pregnant wife had been raped and killed by a French trapper named Pierre on the *Black River*. The trapper is supposed to have left a button off a tunic to implicate a Mountie. Nelson was supposed to have dragged his wife's body with him all winter until it became warm enough to bury her.

---

*This case was investigated by Const. M. Chappuis and Const. A. Nicolson of the Saskatchewan Provincial Police.

Eleven

Murderer

MUCH DEPENDS ON the origin of the five pieces of gold dental work found in Albert Johnson's pocket before a basic premise can be devised on the question of whether Johnson had killed anyone before he shot King, Millen, and Hersey. If the gold dental work was not his, it would imply that he was a "collector". Then it would follow that the man was either a grave robber or a murderer, with the weight tending to fall on the side of the latter. If, on the other hand, the dental work was his, he would be partially vindicated on the above point.

Staff Sgt. Terry Shaw of the *R.C.M.P. Quarterly* informed the author that he understood that the pieces of dental work were apparently not Johnson's, but because the case has been in "mothballs" for so many years the report on the dental work is not presently available. A query written to the Depot Division and to the R.C.M.P. museum in Regina revealed that the museum does not have the dental work, the alluvial gold, or the pearls. It was found that these articles reverted to the Crown and were sold.

Dr. D. W. Bellinger, a dentist in Whitehorse, was asked to draw up a dental chart based on Dr. Urquhart's report covering Johnson's teeth. The chart shows six extractions, any one of which could have used a bridge. This leaves a number of gaps—and five dentures.* It would seem likely, then, that if the dental bridges were not Johnson's he would have thrown them away during the chase.

There is a possibility that somewhere along the line the trapper became involved in a poker game with a logger or prospector and won the dentures as part of a wager. Stranger things have occurred, but gold teeth do not normally become part of a poker "pot", even for those who tend to become eccentric after spending many years in the bush. There is also a chance that he might have stolen the pieces of gold from someone.

If Johnson was a killer, were there any victims, and if so, where? Such a question would be almost impossible to answer at the time of Johnson's death. Communications were too poor, and the territory of Johnson's wanderings too wide, for an accurate appraisal of deaths occurring in the region. A good example of this is that in the case of seven deaths in the Yukon uncovered by the author, not one, including that of Albert Johnson, is on record in

*See Appendix "A", Exhibits "A" and "D", for dental information.

Yukon's Department of Vital Statistics. (Johnson's death was recorded at Aklavik.) Men who disappeared in the wilderness are *presumed* to have become victims of the dangers inherent in living in the bush, or to have succumbed due to health factors, if their disappearances were heard about at all. In such cases, it was almost impossible for legal authorities to keep track of foul play because communications were so poor that the death of a man would go unreported for as long as five years. By the time a policeman could check up on the body, there was nothing available but a skeleton, and more often than not the bones would be scattered around the countryside, if found at all.

An occasional death has been reported here and there along Nelson's route, but because these were isolated incidents, and communications were poor, no pattern emerged at the time which would point to Arthur Nelson's involvement.

Headless Valley and the South Nahanni Murders*

The South Nahanni River is located in the southwest corner of the Northwest Territories. Headless Valley is part of the Nahanni Valley, and is downstream from 315-feet-high Virginia Falls, the highest waterfall of consequential volume of flow in North America. The Flat River, which is a tributary of the South Nahanni, flows into the larger river between the falls and Headless Valley. Headless Valley received its name because of a number of bodies or skulls discovered in the Nahanni region over the years. Several of the bodies were found in the Nahanni Valley, though most were found along the Flat River Valley.

*Headless Valley was originally called Deadman's Valley.

Over the years numerous explanations have been given in attempts to point up the reason for the killings in the area and the disappearance of the heads, but most were quite vague. Before now, no one ever advanced the theory that the heads might have been purposely removed with robbery the motive! It follows that if Albert Johnson was in possession of pieces of gold dental work which were not his, and that if he and Arthur Nelson were the same person, Nelson may have been responsible for some of the killings in the Nahanni region. It should be remembered that Nelson lived only forty miles from the headwaters of the South Nahanni during the years he roamed the regions of the upper Macmillan River. If Nelson was a killer and was stealing his victim's teeth, he would naturally remove the head, knowing that discoverers of the body would immediately suspect foul play if the skull was found to be lacking gold teeth or to have been tampered with. He would also know that any man murdered in such a wilderness would have his body picked clean by ravens, camp robbers, and assorted flesh-eating mammals within a matter of weeks. This would adequately disguise any evidence of wrongdoing.

Since Nelson did not appear in the north country until 1926, he cannot be blamed for all the killings and disappearances in the Nahanni country.

The chief cause of the Nahanni–Headless Valley "legend" was the finding of the headless skeletons of William and Frank McLeod ninety miles up the Nahanni River by a party of five prospectors in 1908, four years after the McLeods and a man by the name of Robert Weir went into the region to trap, hunt, and prospect. A headless skeleton presumed to be Robert Weir was later found on the headwaters of the Flat River by Upper Liard Indians. This gave rise to the legend of the "Lost McLeod Mine", as rumours attributed their death to robbers who killed them for the gold they presumably had mined in the region.

Legends concerning these deaths served to publicize the

legend of the "Lost McLeod Mine", which Nelson probably hunted for.

The accounts of the deaths in the Nahanni area are largely question marks. The Mounties themselves admit that there is a possibility of a number of deaths occurring in the region which they never heard about, or which, if they did hear about them, they were not able to verify.

The Nahanni region has a peculiar location. The South Nahanni River and the Flat River, though technically under the jurisdiction of the Northwest Territories, run parallel to what was an uninhabited region close to the border of the Yukon Territory. Access to the area drained by the two rivers was so diverse that a man going into the country from Fort Simpson on the Mackenzie River would never be aware of a man entering the region via the headwaters of the Ross River in the Yukon Territory or by way of the Hyland River from Watson Lake, Y.T., or Lower Post, British Columbia.

This, of course, created all sorts of jurisdictional problems in relation to matters involving the law, and must have caused members of the R.C.M.P. many frustrating moments through the years. Today a road runs to the Canadian Tungsten Company mine on the upper reaches of the Flat River, but until the 1960s no such road existed.

Arthur Nelson arrived in Ross River in the summer of 1927. That same summer another mystery evolved when the body of Charles Taylor, alias "Yukon" Fisher, was reported to have been found by a "Captain" Knox near the headwaters of the Flat River. The position of his remains indicated that he may have attempted to defend himself but had been killed in the process. He may even have been killed by a bear; a grizzly's skeleton was found near him, and he might have shot the bear and then been killed by it. No motives were established in the case, since Taylor's cabin was burned to the ground, thus effectively disguising whether a theft took place.

If Arthur Nelson was involved in the Taylor killing

there were no witnesses to the fact, nor have any witnesses come forward who ever saw him in the Flat River area. Taylor is known to have traded his furs at the Ross River trading post, and also to have purchased supplies with coarse gold nuggets which he supposedly acquired while prospecting. If Nelson travelled to Ross River from Dease Lake via the Hyland River it would have been possible for him to have killed Taylor on the upper Flat River before crossing to the headwaters of the Pelly and descending to the Ross River post, although it would be a roundabout route.

The next party to meet with any difficulties in the Nahanni region was that consisting of Angus Hall, James Gilroy, and Andrew Hay. The three men made their way up the South Nahanni River in May 1929. May is a poor month to travel in the Nahanni area because the river usually goes into flood at this time of the year. The three men were continually harassed by rising waters as storms swept the area. As a result, they decided to climb over the height of land between Scow and Bennett creeks to Bennett Creek, where they planned to prospect for gold. A small conflict arose between Hall on the one hand and Hay and Gilroy on the other. Hall felt that the other men were not travelling light enough and were moving too slowly for him. He told them that he would go ahead to Bennett Creek where he would make camp and start work on a cabin. He walked over a crest of a ridge above Hay and Gilroy, and was never seen again. A footprint was discovered in the Bennett Creek valley which could have been made by Hall, or it may have been made by R. M. Patterson, who was in the area the year before and wrote in his book *Dangerous River* that it might have been his footprint. The footprint may also have been made by someone with more aggressive designs than those of other men. In other words, Nelson could have done the job of obliterating Hall. Again, snowslides, an irritable grizzly, or soft river ice could have done the same thing. No one will ever know.

It should be pointed out that a man such as Nelson, who never said a word to anyone about where he had been, or where he was going, could have been capable of causing an unbelievable amount of trouble if he was dedicated to the occupations of theft and murder. Chuck Allen, who once trapped at Sheldon Lake, which is located forty miles from the headwaters of the South Nahanni River, told the author that a man could walk from the lower reaches of the Flat River to Sheldon Lake and the upper Macmillan in less than a week if he was in good condition. Allen himself had been flown into the Rat River and had walked back to Sheldon Lake in two weeks, hunting beaver as he went. Alan Kulan, discoverer of the Anvil mine, and a man who has walked over much of the country covered by Arthur Nelson, believes it would not be difficult for a man in good shape to make the 120-mile trip in four days, especially when the snow is packed hard in the winter.

The Nahanni mysteries deepened when the charred remains of Phil Powers were found in the bunk of his burned-out cabin far up the Flat River in the fall of 1932. Powers went into the Nahanni country to prospect and trap in the spring of 1931. Albert Faille discovered Powers' remains in the summer of 1932, but the discovery was not officially investigated until the fall. A note in pencil on one of his cache posts read simply "Finis—1932—Phil Powers". There seems no doubt that the writing was Powers', and the clear meaning appeared to be suicide, but the crushing of his skull by the fallen timbers of the burned cabin made the manner of his death uncertain, and it remains a minor mystery.

It must be pointed out here that Arthur Nelson crossed the mountains to the Arctic slope from Keno, Y.T., on May 7, 1931, and consequently would seem to be exonerated in the Powers case, *if* it were possible to pin down the date of Powers' arrival in the Flat River country. So the situation repeats itself. Could Powers have been told at gun point to write the 1932 inscription on the cache to make it look like suicide, and then been murdered? Afterwards, was his body placed in the bunk, and his head crushed to make it look as though a falling log had done the job?

Upper Macmillan Disappearances

The Powers case was the last in the Nahanni region in which Nelson could have had a hand, but concurrently there were a number of disappearances in the vicinity of the headwaters of the Macmillan River. Dan Gleason, of Keno, Y.T., disappeared on the Hess River in the fall of 1926. He had been on a prospecting trip on the headwaters of Russell Creek where Arthur Nelson was later to live. The last man to see Gleason alive was Lt.-Col. Neville Armstrong, who was attempting to set up a hydraulic operation along Russell Creek at that time. Armstrong said that Gleason told him he was going overland from Russell Creek to the Hess River in an effort to find a cross-country route to Robert Levac's trading post at Fraser Falls. Remains of his last camp were found eight miles above the confluence of the Hess and Stewart rivers. The popular consensus of opinion was that he built a raft and the raft overturned in the rapids near that point, and the man drowned. Gleason's body was never found. Nelson probably had nothing to do with Gleason's death, having only first arrived in Ross River in 1927. On the other hand, his comings and goings were of so mysterious a nature there was no telling where he *could* have been.

Still another strange disappearance occurred on October 5, 1928, when Dawson's leading physician, Dr. J. O. La-Chapelle, and a woman from Keno by the name of Elizabeth Ray, and a woodcutter by the name of John Timson embarked in LaChapelle's canoe for a seventy-five-mile trip from Stewart Island to Dawson City on the Yukon River. LaChapelle had dinner with Gerald and Rose Kelley the night before he undertook the trip. They warned him that he was taking a chance because the river was running heavy in ice. LaChapelle laughed off the advice by saying he had always made it before. He left with his two companions the next morning. The canoe was found overturned at the mouth of Henderson slough about six miles down the Yukon River. No sign of the three people was ever seen again, but the mystery did not end there. The doctor's pet cocker spaniel, Rufus, was found alive along the banks of Henderson slough, and the canoe on close inspection was found to have a hole made in it from the inside outwards. Rumours persisted that a fourth person was never reported missing. Since no one knows where Nelson was except for part of the summer and fall of 1928, the question arises of whether he could have had something to do with the disappearance of the LaChapelle party. Since Timson was a woodcutter, Nelson may have had something to do with Timson's woodcutting operation. Itinerant woodchoppers arrived and departed like the leaves of autumn along the Yukon River in the days of the wood-burning steamboats. And whether Nelson worked for Timson has been impossible to ascertain. One item was brought to light by veteran reporter Archie Gillespie, who said Miss Ray was carrying a small fortune in jewels when she disappeared.

All but a few of those incidents already mentioned were recalled by wilderness residents and were not officially recorded in either the Yukon's or the Northwest Territories' Departments of Vital Statistics. This being the case, how many more individuals have been killed or have disappeared over the years of whom there is no record or recollection at all! This points up the fact that if a demented man wanted to murder and plunder lonely trappers and prospectors for their gold, furs, money, and other valuables, it would have been relatively easy to get away with in those days.

An argument in favour of the view that Nelson may have been a predator on his fellow man was his penchant for out-of-the-way places that indicated activity of some sort. He tramped to Thibert Creek, B.C., the scene of a small gold rush. He went to Sheldon Lake, Y.T., which is on the main trail between the Northwest Territories and the Yukon Territory, as well as being the crossroads between the headwaters of the Macmillan River and the valley of the South Nahanni. He drifted over to the area drained by Russell Creek, which was also the scene of a small stampede. Later, under the name of Albert Johnson, he built a cabin on the Rat River, which for centuries had been the main portage route between the Yukon River drainage and the Mackenzie River system. Why would so unsociable a person seek out such locations if he wanted to avoid people? There are abundant out-of-the-way places where a man could go about his business with little fear of running into anyone. On the other hand, if Nelson (i.e. Johnson) was a "highwayman" or a pirate as they call such a person on the high seas, he would seek "routes of trade" which he could plunder while at the same time leaving himself a good chance to go undetected.

One incongruity supporting the plundering suggestion is that Nelson waited for the supply boat in Ross River for a month during the summer of 1928, and though he had plenty of time, did not sell his furs at the Ross River post. Instead, he journeyed over two hundred miles during the same summer to sell them in Mayo to another branch of the identical store, Taylor and Drury. Why did Nelson do this unless he was afraid that the real owner's style of making fur stretchers and skinning animals would be recognized by Roy Buttle as not being Nelson's?

118

At this point it should be made clear that not all the evidence is damning with regard to Arthur Nelson. To be completely fair, proper weight should be given to many misrepresentations and interpretations which have tended to place Nelson in a more sinister light than he may deserve.

One consistent misinterpretation is that the $2,410 in cash found on Johnson was an unusual amount of money to find on a trapper in 1932.* It was not. Marten (sable) prices at that time approached the hundred-dollar mark. Good cross fox furs brought $500. Arctic fox furs brought a high price. It was not unusual for a trapper to make $5,000 during a winter season, and on one occasion two trappers sold their furs for $50,000 in Mayo. The significance of this would seem to favour Johnson's being nothing other than what he appeared to be—a trapper and prospector.

Another misconception is that Johnson was in violation of the law when he tripped traps found on what he considered his trap line. On the contrary, springing traps and hanging them on a bush was the accepted practice on a trap line under dispute during the days before installation of registered trap lines.

Some have held that Johnson was a violator of the licensing law for trapping. This may have been true, but Earl Hersey told the author in a letter that the general consensus of opinion of many of the trappers who were involved in the hunt was that Johnson thought he had crossed into the Yukon Territory where there was no need for a licence, it being on the hunting ticket.

Another aspect of the case which should be put into proper perspective is the belief that the sawed-off barrel of the shotgun and the sawed-off stock of the .22 rifle repre-

*The names Johnson and Nelson are used interchangeably. For the purpose of simplification, Nelson is called Johnson north of the Arctic slope.

sented implements of a killer or a bandit. Actually, there is a more practical reason for cutting these down and that is to lessen the weight and increase the facility of carrying the weapons in a man's pack. These two firearms, plus the 30-30 Savage, have their utility in the bush. It was not uncommon for a trapper to carry a shortened .22, and though a sawed-off 16-gauge was unusual, it would be of value in shooting birds.

A false impression has been conveyed through the years suggesting that Johnson had built a "cabin-fortress", the "pit" of the structure being considered an ominous inclusion. Reports of anthropologists effectively debunk this idea. The "pit-house" or "pit-cabin" has been used by Eskimos and Indians for centuries, and in various areas it is common among white people. Considering the fact that pit-cellars are dug in most cabins anyway in order to keep food from freezing, it is not unusual for the whole cabin to be countersunk in the earth for warmth.

Loopholes in the moss chinking of the Johnson cabin were reported by the Mounties to have been punched *after* Johnson shot King, not before as has been stated in exaggerations which have developed about the case.

Such are the pros and cons of the "Mad Trapper's" activities. Speculation has continued through the years and the argument over whether or not Albert Johnson was a villain still rages whenever dwellers of the north country get together.

Twelve

Or Victim?

WHEN ALL IS said, it may be that Johnson was basically an honest man who became enmeshed in a series of events which, once commenced, could bring about nothing but his downfall. Const. Edgar Millen, a true northern hero in every sense of the word, was caught up in this same stream that led to his death as well. Once events were set in motion, the situation inexorably compounded and dealt catastrophe to those entrapped in it.

In reviewing the over-all picture of the twentieth-century fur trade, with high fur prices running parallel to an over-all depression, it is a miracle that this type of confrontation had not occurred more often and much sooner. That it had not is a lasting tribute to the skill which the Mounted Police displayed in patrolling the north.

The late twenties saw the beginning of the "big depression". There was still a huge agrarian population in both the United States and Canada. Farm prices hit rock bottom, causing young men to leave the family ranch and scatter to the four winds seeking employment and a wage. As the depression deepened, even this source of funds disappeared. This caused a few farm boys who had run trap lines on their fathers' homesteads in earlier days to head north where they had heard fabulous prices were being paid for mink, marten, and Arctic fox. If they did not make out in the winter, they could always prospect for gold in the summer. Above all, they could survive with little cash.

Many of these men were not suited for running a trap line in a land where temperatures range down to seventy-five below zero and one man might not see another for six months. Thus, as these men drifted north, ignoring lopsticks and barging in on established trap lines, they caused considerable confusion and consternation among Indian and white trappers who had been working at the occupation for years.* This resentment was also reflected among the traders, who naturally enough felt that their duty was to remain loyal to the men who had proven themselves to be good trappers over the years.

Since there were no laws governing assignment of a trapping territory, a trapper took his complaint to the nearest detachment of the R.C.M.P. when he figured his rights were being infringed upon. The Mounties settled amicably

---

*For a review of this situation see *Annual Report of the Department of Indian Affairs*, March 1936, King's Printer, Ottawa, p. 13.

thousands of such disputes, which were not publicized because a crime was prevented. Only committed crimes, not averted ones, reach the pages of history. It was for these reasons that Const. Millen first moved into the Albert Johnson orbit, in response to a request to check the man out—mainly to see that he could handle himself in the country.

It must be remembered that when Nelson first appeared in the north country—in northern British Columbia—Ed Asp gave him permission to use the upper end of his trap line. And again, when the itinerant trapper went to Mayo, Jim Mervyn made a deal with him wherein Mervyn approved Nelson's using his trap line. The winter following this, Nelson trapped far up the Macmillan River, so that when he appeared one night to be studying Arthur John's and Jinx Johnnie's movements with a jaundiced eye, it may have been that he was worried about their trapping in "his" territory.

In other words, without a registered trap line drawn on a map, as is the custom and the law today, the old system encouraged a sort of chaos which all but ensured dispute sooner or later.

At Fort McPherson, it was probably Johnson's vagueness in his answers to Millen concerning his destination that planted a seed of distrust in the back of Millen's mind. The Mountie was popular in the north country and was known for being a fair person, who could be expected to lean towards protecting the local trappers while administering justice.

Johnson, a quiet and withdrawn man, may have been vague—not by design, but by the very nature of his being. It must be recalled that the men who knew Johnson in the Yukon—those who really knew him best—liked and trusted him. Just because a man is silent does not mean that he cannot be friendly, but to the average citizen a quiet man is an enigma. His silence usually rankles those who meet him. *Homo sapiens* is a social being, and any man who goes against the grain by walking around in a shell of silence is often considered to have had a "past". So it was with Johnson wherever he appeared. His silence was not "normal", so it was believed that he might have been a law breaker, especially since he showed a certain dislike of law men. However, this was often true of working "stiffs", such as loggers and miners, who often found themselves face to face with the law in labour disputes. On top of this, Johnson may have been an illegal immigrant, which would give further cause for avoiding the law and being silent about his past.

Bishop Geddes, of the Anglican Church, may have been overly protective in reporting Johnson's presence at Fort McPherson. Geddes was a former chaplain in the British army and had served in the First World War. He had been with Inspector Eames on Herschel Island, and when the police moved their sub-district headquarters to Aklavik, he moved also. Geddes, according to many white and Indian residents of the north country, was inclined to be overly paternal in dealing with his "flock". Though well-intended, this policy was bound to irritate some people.

Albert Johnson might have walked into a situation which was slightly intolerant of his presence, though he, in ignorance, would never have known this. Antipathy may have boiled under cover and never would have surfaced except under a veil of platitudes.

The same paternalistic attitude can be laid on the doorstep of the fur traders. They too, tended to take a fatherly interest in the affairs of the men with whom they dealt, and were not above suggesting that an unwanted man be harassed to a point where he moved on to another location.

These sorts of things had happened in other areas; whether they pertained in Albert Johnson's case is only supposition, of course.

Still another "climate" into which Johnson moved was a general bitterness on the part of the Indians over the trapping and hunting laws imposed on them by the white men. The Indians often trapped when they saw fit without bothering to investigate laws governing their actions. Indeed, one old-timer, now dead, insisted to the author that many Indians started trapping that winter before the season opened and that Johnson possibly was quietly enforcing the law by springing traps! If such was the case, Johnson should have reported the violations to the police. However, Johnson's withdrawn nature suggests that he would never have solicited the help of an agency which he already distrusted. The principles of the law and its official servants are not necessarily the same to many people.

As has been previously mentioned, Albert Johnson showed himself to be an extremely nervous man. If Johnson was an Army veteran he very well may have been shell-shocked. More men were shell-shocked in the trenches of the First World War than in all the other wars fought before or since. A shell-shock victim is not noticeable to the "naked eye". He can go for years and apparently be as normal as the next person, but in periods of sudden stress he has a tendency to temporarily fall apart.

This then was the over-all situation in December 1931 when William Nerysoo complained to Const. Edgar Millen, commanding the Arctic Red River post, that Johnson had been interfering with his trap line. Millen, with seeds of distrust of Johnson already in his mind from their meeting the previous summer, told Const. King to investigate the complaint.

It must not have been a very pleasant task for King to go out on the trail on Boxing Day to investigate an eccentric living eighty miles out in the bush. On December 28, King had his first confrontation with Albert Johnson. He saw smoke coming out of the Johnson cabin and spent an hour finding out that Johnson would have nothing to do with him. Johnson said not a word the entire time King was there. Here, some people may raise the question that

Johnson possibly was hard of hearing and may not have heard King. If this fact were true, no one in either the Northwest Territories, the Yukon Territory, or northern British Columbia ever noticed it. King said that he saw Johnson peering at him through the window, which would apparently undercut any argument that Johnson might have placed a green log on the fire and been out on his trap line when King visited the cabin the first time. If Johnson had not been in the cabin the first time, it would have provided a more logical reason for what happened later. King then mushed to Aklavik to obtain a warrant, was given reinforcements in the persons of McDowell and his assistant, and then raced back to Rat River. According to Frank Riddell, who was interviewed on the CBC, the men were invited to a party at the Hudson's Bay Company post at Fort McPherson. King had this in his mind when he and McDowell were mushing south, and King figured they could easily get to McPherson by New Year's Eve if they reached Johnson's place by noon.

The important point here is that the furthest thing from the policemen's minds at this time was harassment. They were in a hurry to get Johnson's story and to move on.

Some thought should be given to Johnson's frame of mind at this time. He was a silent man who lived alone and had been living that way for at least five years. It was the holiday season. Psychiatrists have frequently pointed out that more people commit suicide at this time of the year than at any other. In other words, if there was a time for Johnson to be in a state of depression, this would be it. Who knows what fond memories he may have had of Christmases long past? No man can ever escape his memories; no matter how far he may go, the nostalgia of the past will always be with him. So he sat there, possibly thinking of happier days, at the same time contemplating the fact that a Mountie was most surely coming back with a warrant to search his cabin and talk with him. No one will ever know just what were Johnson's thoughts when King knocked on the door. It would seem that if Johnson meant to shoot King, he would have planned it and waylaid the Mounties on the trail. On the other hand, he may have figured that his cabin was a good fortress and that if he was going to do any shooting it would be best from the sanctuary and warmth provided by his shack.

Since Johnson was apparently involved in a trap line hassle, he more than likely kept a loaded rifle within easy reach of his bunk. If he had been asleep when King knocked on the door, and was of a nervous nature, he may have literally woken up shooting.

In capsulizing the issues, one fact must be faced: Johnson was guilty of shooting Constable King. No matter what his complaint could have been, he was subject to prosecution. Even after he shot King, it must be remembered that Inspector Eames advised him that King was alive and he would not be placed on trial for murder.

The trapper chose to fight it out, and in so doing, demonstrated that he was either obsessively bent on self-destruction, or hiding something in his past which he knew doomed him if he did surrender. Whether the Mounties killed a lone "gone mad" trapper, or a ruthless killer, or whether Albert Johnson was the hapless victim of a series of unfortunate circumstances, are unanswered questions which are now a part of the lore of that raw, mysterious land of the great Arctic forests.

Bibliography

Books

ANDERSON, FRANK. *The Death of Albert Johnson*. Edmonton: Frontier Publishing Co., 1968.

ARMSTRONG, MAJOR A. D. *After Big Game in the Upper Yukon*. London: John Long Ltd., 1937.

BERTON, PIERRE. *Klondike*. Toronto: McClelland & Stewart, 1958.

BOND, JAMES H. *From Out of the Yukon*. Portland: Binfords & Mort, 1948.

CAMPBELL, ROBERT. *Journals*. Seattle: J. P. Bindery, 1958.

CAMSELL, CHARLES. *Son of the North*. Toronto: Ryerson, 1954.

CHASE, WILLIAM H. *Reminiscences of Captain Billy Moore*. Kansas City: Burton Publishing Co., 1947.

FERGUSON, CHICK. *Mink, Mary and Me*. New York: M. S. Mill, 1946.

FETHERSTONHAUGH, W. A. *The Royal Canadian Mounted Police*. Garden City: Garden City Publishing Co., 1938.

GODSELL, PHILIP. *Pilots of the Purple Twilight*. Toronto: Ryerson Press, 1955.

GRAHAM, ANGUS. *The Golden Grindstone—The Adventures of George M. Mitchell*. London: Chatto & Windus, 1936.

LARGE, R. G. *The Skeena*. Vancouver: Mitchell Press, 1957.

LONGSTRETH, J. MORRIS. *The Silent Force*. New York: Century, 1927.

MACGREGOR, J. G. *The Klondike Rush Through Edmonton*. Toronto: McClelland & Stewart, 1970.

ONRAET, TONY. *Sixty Below*. New York: Didier, 1948.

PAGE, ELIZABETH. *Wild Horses and Gold: From Wyoming to the Yukon*. New York: Farrar & Rinehart, 1932.

PATTERSON, R. M. *Finlay's River*. Toronto: Macmillan, 1968.

———. *Trail to the Interior*. Toronto: Macmillan, 1966.

———. *Dangerous River*. Sidney: Gray's, 1966.

PEAKE, FRANK A. *The Bishop Who Ate His Boots*. Toronto: Anglican Church of Canada, 1966.

SELOUS, F. C. *Hunting Trips in North America*. New York: Scribner's, 1907.

SHELDON, CHARLES. *The Wilderness of the Upper Yukon*. Toronto: Copp Clark, 1911.

STEFANSSON, VILHJALMUR. *The Friendly Arctic*. New York: Macmillan, 1921.

TOLLEMACHE, HON. STRATFORD. *Reminiscences of the Yukon*. Toronto: Wm. Briggs, 1912.

Government Documents

CANADA. Department of Indian Affairs. *Annual Report*. Ottawa: King's Printer, 1936.

CANADA. Geological Survey. George M. Dawson. *Report of an Exploration in the Yukon District of 1887*. Ottawa: Queen's Printer, 1898.

CANADA. Geological Survey. H. S. Bostock, ed. *Selected Field Reports of the Geological Survey of Canada*. Ottawa: Queen's Printer, 1957.

CANADA. Geological Survey. W. A. Johnston. "Gold Placers of the Dease Lake Area", *Summary Report, 1925 Part A*. Ottawa: King's Printer, 1926.

CANADA, Royal Canadian Signals. Report, 1932.

Periodicals

Alaska Sportsman, January 1964.

Maclean's Magazine, October 1, 1955.

R.C.M.P. Quarterly, October 1960.

True Detective Mysteries Magazine, October, November, 1932.

Whitehorse Star, June 1929.

Appendix "A"

Exhibit "A"

FROM THE OFFICE of the Commissioner, Royal Canadian Mounted Police, Ottawa, dated November 24, 1969, to the author:

Dear Sir:

Your recent request for information on the Albert Johnson case has been referred to this office by Chief Superintendent Stone, Commanding "Depot" Division.

We are unable to locate the Death Certificate or a copy of Johnson's fingerprints, however, we are enclosing xerox copies of the Inquisition form, Information to Hold Inquest and Warrant to Bury form, that may be of interest to you. We are also imbodying hereunder a full description of Albert Johnson which contains considerable detail on his teeth.

"Height: 5' 9" to 5' 9½"; Chest: 34"; Estimated Weight: 145 to 150 lbs.; Light brown hair; beginning to recede on forehead, light brown beard and moustache — beard and moustache less than a month old; pale blue eyes; snubbed, upturned nose; moderate prominence of cheek bones; ears definitely lobed; low-set and close to head; small wart or mole 2 inches to left of spine, mid-lumbar region; this is only natural mark on body. There are no operation scars or evidence of old fractures; apparent age: 35 to 40 years; Teeth: well cared for, numerous fillings, though obviously neglected for a period of some months; Left upper jaw; third molar and wisdom tooth extracted: silver filling second molar, gold filling second incisor. Right upper jaw: first molar extracted. Second molar, large cavity, anterior surface where filling has dropped out, bicuspid also extracted. Left lower jaw; second and third molars extracted. Right lower jaw: bicuspid crowned with gold to which is attached gold bridge reaching back to third molar which is also gold crowned; wisdom tooth extracted. Feet approximately 9½ inches long."

We are also enclosing a photograph of Johnson after his death, one of Inspector Eames, two aerial shots of the Eagle River area where Johnson was shot, one of Cpl. King, that we hope will be suitable for your purpose.

Yours truly,
(Sgn.) G. A. Potts, Insp.,
Liaison Officer.

Exhibit "B"

INQUISITION

CANADA: Northwest Territories. An inquisition indented taken for our Sovereign Lord the King at the R.C.M. Police Barracks, Aklavik in the North-West Territories on the 18th. day of February A.D. 1932 before Dr. J. A. Urquhart, M.D. one of the Coroners of our said Lord the King for the said Northwest Territories on view of the body of a man known as Albert Johnson then and there lying dead, upon the oath or affirmation of C. G. Matthews, J. Parsons, L. Scott-Brown, I. Neary, N. H. Hancock and R. G. Kilgour, good and lawful men of the said Northwest Territories, duly chosen, and who being then and there duly sworn, and charged to inquire for our said Lord the King, when, where, how and by what means the said man known as Albert Johnson came to his death, do upon their oath say: That we, the Jury, find that the man known as Albert Johnson came to his death from concentrated rifle fire from a party composed of members of the Royal Canadian Mounted Police and others, Johnson having been called upon to surrender by several members of the party and still desperately resisting arrest we are satisfied that no responsibility rests with any member of the party or the party as a whole. We are further satisfied from the evidence that the party had no other means of effecting Johnson's capture except by the method employed.

In witness whereof, as well the said Coroners as the jurors aforesaid, have hereunto set and subscribed their hands and seals the day and year first above written.

(Sgd) J. A. Urquhart	Coroner.
(Sgd) C. G. Matthews,	Juror.
(Sgd) I. Neary,	Juror.
(Sgd) N. E. Hancock,	Juror.
(Sgd) R. H. Kilgour,	Juror.
(Sgd) J. Parsons,	Juror.
(Sgd) L. Scott-Brown.	Juror.

Exhibit "C"

Privy Council, Canada

Certified to be a true copy of a Minute of a Meeting of the Committee of the Privy Council, approved by His Excellency the Administrator on the 20th February, 1940.

The Committee of the Privy Council have had before them a report, dated February 8th, 1940, from the Minister of Finance and the Minister of Mines and Resources, stating:

THAT ALBERT JOHNSON of Rat River, in the Northwest Territories, a trapper, commonly known as the "Mad Trapper," was killed in the said Territories on the 17th day of February, 1932, while eluding capture by the Royal Canadian Mounted Police;

THAT this said man's estate was placed in the hands of Mr. H. Milton Martin, Public Administrator for the District of Mackenzie in the Northwest Territories, for administration, in accordance with the Ordinances of the Northwest Territories in that behalf;

THAT in the course of administration it became apparent, after thorough search, that the said Albert Johnson died leaving no heirs or next of kin him surviving, in consequence whereof the said estate would fall into His Majesty the King in right of Canada as bonavacantia.

THAT the Public Administrator, pursuant to the Order of the Stipendiary Magistrate of the 28th day of February, 1939, paid over to the Receiver General of Canada the sum of One Thousand Seven Hundred and Forty-eight Dollars and Forty Cents ($1748.40) as the balance of liquid assets of the estate after payment of all proper costs, charges and debts and accounts taken;

THAT the articles set out in the attached schedule, assets other than liquid assets of the said estate, are presently in the hands of His Majesty;

THAT the Commissioner of the Royal Canadian Mounted Police reports that with the exception of the articles in sections (a) and (b) of the schedule listed, all the articles set out in the said schedule have no value and might without loss to His Majesty be destroyed;

THAT the said Commissioner further reports that the articles set out in section (b) of the said schedule have a laboratory value to the Royal Canadian Mounted Police and requests that authority be sought to place the same in his hands for deposit in the Royal Canadian Mounted Police museum at Regina, Saskatchewan.

The Ministers, therefore, recommend that authority be given to sell the articles listed in section (a) of the schedule attached; to turn over to the Commissioner of the Royal Canadian Mounted Police for laboratory or museum purposes the articles listed in section (b) of the said schedule and to effect the destruction of the articles listed in section (c) of the said schedule.

The Committee concur in the foregoing recommendation and submit the same for approval.

(Sgd) H. W. Lothrop
Acting Clerk of the Privy Council.

Royal Canadian Mounted Police Schedule

List of effects of Albert Johnson — Estate of

(a) (1) small glass bottle containing:
five pearls, approximate value $15.00 and five pieces of gold dental work 4 dwt. approximate value $3.20.

(2) small glass bottle containing:
13 dwt. of alluvial gold, approximate value $9.36. *Articles which it is requested be left with the Royal Canadian Mounted Police for inclusion in the Royal Canadian Mounted Police Museum at Regina, Sask.*

(b) (1) Savage 30-30 Rifle, No. 293575, Model 99.

(2) Iver Johnson Sawed off shot gun, No. 5537XF. 16 ga.

(3) .22 Winchester Rifle, Model 58, No number. Stock sawn off.

(4) Pocket Compass.

(5) Axe – Handle bearing bullet mark.

(6) Sack containing lard tin and lid used as tea pail, showing bullet holes.

Articles of no value, for which authority to destroy is requested.

(c) (1) Knife made from spring trap.

(2) Match safe.

(3) Gillette Safety Razor.

(4) Envelope containing piece of three cornered file; awl made from three cornered file; chisel made from nail.

(5) Small knife made from piece of metal, with moose-skin cover.

(6) Mooseskin Rifle cover.

(7) Mooseskin pouch.

(8) Mooseskin sewing pouch containing needles and thread.

(9) Small spring.

(10) Nails wrapped in tinfoil.

(11) Matches wrapped in tinfoil.

(12) 30-30 Cartridge box containing small empty bottle and pieces of wax.

(13) Sack containing thirty-nine 30-30 shells.
    1 box .22 shells (30)
    1 box .22 shells (30)

(14) Seven pieces of moosehide.

(15) Sack containing six empty sacks;
    15 pieces of babiche.
    1 large bundle of babiche. (snowshoe lacing)
    1 bdle. Sewing thread.
    1 piece mooseskin lace.

(16) Calico rifle cover.

(17) Large envelope containing:

1 box Pony Matches.
1 bndl Sulphur Matches wrapped in tinfoil.
1 bndl Sulphur Matches wrapped in paper.
1 tinfoil packet containing 2 pills.
1 paper package containing six pills.
1 paper package containing fish hooks.
1 tinfoil package containing oily rag.
1 leather cover containing comb and sewing materials.
1 paper and tinfoil package containing grey powder.
1 rag bundle containing twine.
1 rag bundle containing sewing twine.
1 paper package containing 24 pills.
1 paper package containing fish hooks.
4 .22 shells
4 – 16 ga. Shot Gun Shells.
1 Moosehide folder containing mirror.
1 rag containing pepper.
1 sack containing salt.

Exhibit "D"

FROM THE Savage Arms Co., Westfield, Mass., dated Nov. 4, 1969, to the author:

In reply to your inquiry of October 31, 1969, regarding a Savage 30-30 Serial #293575.

Our records show this to be a Model 99-30-30F, the "F" indicating it to be a featherweight model. The record also shows that this rifle was shipped on May 2, 1927, to Marshall Wells Company. We still do business with Marshall Wells Limited in Canada, which I am sure is the same company.

The letter is signed by Robert McComb, Works Manager of the Savage Arms Division of the Emhart Corporation.

Marshall Wells' largest customer in the north country was Taylor and Drury, and indications are that the rifle was purchased at Ross River, Yukon Territory.

Exhibit "E"

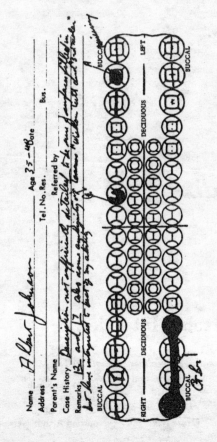

Dental Chart of Johnson

DRAWN UP BY Dr. Pugh of Whitehorse on basis of Mountie description furnished author. See Exhibit "A".

Appendix "B"

Personal Interviews

(Unless otherwise noted, all localities are in the Yukon.)

ALLEN, CHUCK	*Deceased*	Trail to the South Nahanni.
ANDISON, JACK	*Elsa*	Trail to Lansing.
ASP (FAMILY)	*Dease Lake, B.C.*	Notes on Arthur Nelson.

HAGER, EDWIN, MARY, JULIUS	*Mayo*	Mayo; Loucheux Indian history.
HAWTHORNE, JACK	*Mayo*	Background—Keno, Mayo.
HAYDON, JOHN	*Whitehorse*	Description Husky Dog River area.
HENDERSON, CHESTER	*Dawson City*	General Yukon history.
HENRY, JOE AND ANNIE	*Dawson City*	History of Loucheux people.
HERSEY, EARL	*Barrie, Ont.*	Pursuit of Johnson; final battle.
HOLMBERG, SWEDE	*Whitehorse*	Nelson at Dease Lake.
HUTCHINSON, BILL	*Whitehorse*	Yukon history since 1913.
INNES-TAYLOR, ALAN	*Whitehorse*	Nelson's boat; Tatondik River.
ISAAC, SAM	*Pelly Crossing*	Conversation with Arthur Nelson.
JACK, SCAMBELLA	*Carmacks*	Nelson at Sheldon Lake; identify photo.
JOHN, ARTHUR	*Ross River*	Description of Arthur Nelson.
JOHNNIE, LONNIE	*Mayo*	Nelson at Lansing.
KAZINSKY, LOUIS	*Mayo*	Background—Keno, Mayo.
KENDI, MRS. JULIUS	*Mayo*	Peel and Wind rivers history.
KRAUS, GUS	*Nahanni, N.W.T.*	Account of Gus Leafie.
KULAN, AL	*Vancouver, B.C.*	Description Dease region.
KUNNEZI, MRS. ELIZABETH	*Ft. McPherson, N.W.T.*	Johnson at Ft. McPherson.
LADUE, JOE	*Ross River*	Anecdotes about Arthur Nelson.
LARSON, ERIC	*Dawson City*	Trapping on Hart and Peel rivers.
LAVOIE, FRENCHY	*Whitehorse*	Friend of Hard Rock MacDonald.
LINDSAY, JOE	*Whitehorse*	Pictures of Ross River.
LUCAS, JOHNSON	*Mayo*	Nelson at Fraser Falls.
MALCOLM, TIM AND JAKE	*Eagle, Alaska*	Nelson at Eagle.
MARTIN, ROBERT	*Mayo*	Trail to Beaver River; Ross River history.

MAY, SID	Kamloops, B.C.	Final shoot-out with Johnson.
MC COMB, ROBERT	Westfield, Mass.	Notes on Savage 30-30 rifle.
MC KAMEY, RAY	Whitehorse	Leads on Nahanni; Dease Lake.
MEASE, CHUCK	Deceased	History of Macmillan River.
MELLOR, JAMES	Dawson City	Investigations Dawson, 1932.
MERVYN, NORMAN	Mayo	Nelson at Lansing.
MILLER, DON	Lower Post, B.C.	Leads—Watson Lake area.
MOI, MRS. LAURA	Dawson City	Daughter of J. V. Sullivan.
NETRO, JOE	Old Crow	Trader at Whitestone River, 1931.
NIEMAN, PAUL	Whitehorse	Trapped Bell, Arctic Red rivers.
O'NEIL, BARRY	Whitehorse	Information on Beaver City.
O'NEIL, JOHN	Whitehorse	Description Russell Creek.
PAGE, MRS. ROSE	Porter Creek	Macmillan notes.
PETERS, GEORGE	Carmacks	Identify photo of Nelson.
POTTS, INSPECTOR G. A.	Ottawa, Ont.	R.C.M.P. death records— Johnson.
ROBIN, SGT. PAUL	Whitehorse	Trails of upper Yukon Territory.
ROLLS, MR. AND MRS. JACK, PHIL	Ross River	Leads in Ross River.
SHAW, S/SGT. TERRY	Ottawa, Ont.	Editor, R.C.M.P. Quarterly.
SLIM, FRANK	Whitehorse	Ross River photos, history.
SMITH, JACK	Whitehorse	Russell Creek description.
STONE, SUPT. R.P.	Regina, Sask.	Information on Johnson artifacts.
SUZE, JOE	Dawson City	Nelson at Eagle.
THOMAS, MRS. JESSIE	Deceased	History Old Crow area.
VAN BIBBER, ALEX	Champaigne	Description Rouge, Hess rivers.
VAN BIBBER, DAN	Watson Lake	Nelson at Russell Creek.
VAN BIBBER, GEORGE	Mayo	Anecdotes on Macmillan history.

WALLINGHAM, DICK	*Mayo*	Leads in Mayo, Keno.
WHEELER, CPL. DAN	*Old Crow*	Pictures, notes on Old Crow.
WHITEHEAD, FRED	*Chicken, Alaska*	Search for Lost Powers Mine.
WINAGE, MIKE	*Dawson City*	History of Hart, Klondike rivers.
WOOD, JIM AND MARGARET	*Whitehorse*	Notes on James Mervyn, and Lansing.
WYHARD, FLORENCE	*Whitehorse*	Files of *Whitehorse Star*.
ZENIUK, MRS. ROSE	*Mayo*	Leads in Mayo, Keno.